SAVAGE HEAT

ROYAL BASTARDS MC BOOK 1

K.L. RAMSEY

ROYAL BASTARDS MC SERIES

Erin Trejo: **Blood Lust**

Chelle C Craze & Eli Abbott: **Bad Like Me**

K Webster: **Koyn**

Esther E. Schmidt: **Petros**

Elizabeth Knox: **Bet On Me**

Glenna Maynard: **Lady & the Biker**

Madison Faye: **Hard Bastard**

CM Genovese: **Frozen Rain**

J. Lynn Lombard: **Blayze's Inferno**

Crimson Syn: **Inked In Vengeance**

B.B. Blaque: **Rotten Apple**

Addison Jane: **Her Ransom**

Izzy Sweet * Sean Moriarty: **Broken Wings**

Nikki Landis: **Ridin' For Hell**

KL Ramsey: **Savage Heat**

M.Merin: **Axel**

Sapphire Knight: **Bastard**

Bink Cummings: **Switch Burn**

Winter Travers: **Playboy**

Linny Lawless: **The Heavy Crown**
Jax Hart: **Desert King**
Elle Boon: **Royally Broken**
Kristine Allen: **Voodoo**
Ker Dukey: **Animal**
KE Osborn: **Defining Darkness**
Shannon Youngblood: **Silver & Lace**

ROYAL BASTARDS MC SITES

ROYAL BASTARDS MC FACEBOOK GROUP

WEBSITE

ROYAL BASTARDS CODE:

PROTECT: The club and your brothers come before anything else and must be protected at all costs.

CLUB is FAMILY.

RESPECT: Earn it & Give it. Respect club law. Respect the patch. Respect your brothers. Disrespect a member and there will be hell to pay.

HONOR: Being patched in is an honor, not a right. Your colors are sacred, not to be left alone, and NEVER let them touch the ground.

OL' LADIES: Never disrespect a member's or brother's Ol'Lady. PERIOD.

CHURCH is MANDATORY.

LOYALTY: Takes precedence overall, including well-being.

HONESTY: Never LIE, CHEAT, or STEAL from another member of the club.

TERRITORY: You are to respect your brother's property and follow their Chapter's club rules.

TRUST: Years to earn it...seconds to lose it.

NEVER RIDE OFF: Brothers do not abandon their family

SAVAGE

Savage watched as his latest failure floated down from the atmosphere back to earth. At least this time the damn parachute deployed and he wouldn't have to start from scratch again to rebuild his rocket. Last time that happened, his boss threw a major fit, telling him to get his shit and clear out of his office. A short week later, his boss was standing on Savage's front porch, proverbial hat in hand, begging him to come back to work. He even gave him some bullshit about the government needing his service and all that shit. Savage didn't have the desire to tell his boss that he had not only served his government for almost twenty years, but he had also had the bullet holes and shrapnel in his leg to prove it.

Sure, he could sit around and complain about his past and waking up every day in pain, but where would that get him. It was his choice to join the Air Force and it was his choice to re-up when he could have gotten out. He saw active combat for the third time and that was when his copter went down and most of his buddies died. There was nothing he could have done differently that day but God, it was just about all he could think about every night when he laid down and tried to sleep. Their faces would flicker through his memories and he knew that he was going to have another restless night ahead. It was who he had become since he was honorably discharged.

Of course, the Army was quick to jump on his specific skill set and make him the best fucking job offer he'd ever gotten. How could he refuse and why would he? He got to stay in Huntsville, Alabama, where his kid could stay in the same school with the only friends she had ever known. Uprooting Chloe wasn't part of his plan—the poor kid hadn't had much stability in her life. Chloe wasn't really his kid, but that wasn't something he liked to think about too often. It brought up too many bad memories and he tried to only look forward, never back.

Savage adopted Chloe when she was just six months old after her mother and father died in a horrible auto accident. She was his niece and when child services showed up at his doorstep with a baby in tow, claiming that his estranged sister had given him full custody in her will, what was he supposed to do? Savage didn't have one fucking idea how to take care of a kid and they were handing him one that still needed twenty-four-seven care. He quickly learned how to change a diaper and what to feed and not feed a six-month-old. Honestly, that last part was learned the hard way because the kid ended up not being able to handle table food at such an early age. Everything he fed her seemed to run through her like sand in a sieve. But, that was all behind him now. He wasn't sure how he would have survived without that little girl. She had become his whole reason for living. Hell, she basically saved his life and gave him purpose and the will to keep going after his accident.

He had only been home for a few months when Chloe came into his life and he was feeling pretty down and sorry for himself. Both of his parents were gone. His father was never really in the picture and his mom died the year he graduated from high school. Her death had sent him into a spiral that led to him joining the Air Force after he graduated. It also was one of the reasons his older sister, Cherry, stopped talking to him. She begged him not to go into the military; even tried to guilt him into feeling bad about leaving her with no one, since both of their parents were gone. But, he didn't listen. Hell, the only thing Savage wanted to do was ride his damn motorcycle and get the fuck out of that town. He was a punk-ass kid who didn't know any better and the day he left to enlist was the last time he saw Cherry alive.

Now, every time he looked at Chloe's sweet face, he saw his sister. He never met Chloe's dad but he had heard that his sister met a good guy and got married. He liked to imagine Cherry happy with her beautiful new family, at least for a little while. She deserved some happiness after all the shit life had thrown at her, including a punk-ass, eighteen-year-old kid brother who thought he knew better than she did. God was he wrong. His relationship with Cherry was the one thing he regretted in life, but Savage learned that regrets would only hold him back and he couldn't allow that. He had too much going for him to wallow in self-pity.

"I think your rocket's a dud." Savage turned to find the hot guy who always seemed to follow him around Redstone Arsenal. It was as if the guy was his personal bodyguard with the way he watched Savage and he had to admit, he wouldn't mind having his body guarded by him.

"Yeah, well, this is literally rocket science, so I can't really use that old line." Savage looked the guy up and down, liking the way he filled out his fatigues. Not having to wear a uniform was one of the many perks of no longer being enlisted. He usually wore ratty old jeans and a t-shirt when he was on base, partially out of defiance but mostly for comfort. The Alabama heat was quite unbearable but he was used to it. He never really lived anywhere else with the exception of being stationed overseas.

"I'm Bowie Wolfe," the guy said, holding out his hand, waiting for Savage to take it.

He shook the younger guy's hand and smiled. "Are you named after the singer?" Savage questioned.

"Yeah," he breathed. "My mother was a huge fan and well, I got stuck with the name."

Savage shrugged, "All in all, I'd say you did alright. David Bowie is a legend, man," he said.

Bowie groaned and laughed. "Yeah, now you just sound like my mother," he teased.

"Thanks for that," Savage grumbled. He knew just by looking at the guy that he had a few years on him. Hell, he had more than a few years but that usually didn't bother him. Savage liked his guys young and feisty.

"Sorry, man. Um, I didn't catch your name," Bowie said.

"Savage," he offered.

"Wow—you gave me shit about my name but yours is pretty epic too. How did you get a name like Savage?" Bowie crossed his arms over his massive chest and waited him out. It wasn't something Savage liked to talk about, but the determination on the guy's face told him he really had no choice in the matter.

"Savage is actually my last name. My first name is Logan, but my club gave me the nickname after I told them about my helicopter going down. Lost a lot of good guys that day and my buddies said I'm still alive because I'm too savage to die."

"You served?" Bowie asked.

"Yeah—career Air Force until the accident and then honorably discharged," Savage admitted. "How about you?" Bowie held his arms wide as if showing Savage his fatigues to prove his point.

"I enlisted in the Army right from high school and haven't left yet. I've been in for twelve years now and I hope to make this my career, but we'll see." Savage did the math in his head and whistled.

"So, you're what—about thirty?" he questioned.

"I'll be thirty-one in a few months," Bowie admitted.

"You're just a kid," Savage teased.

"Yeah—okay, old man," Bowie said. Savage knew the guy was teasing but at forty-five, he was really beginning to feel his age. "And how old are you?" Savage winced at the mention of his age. It was something he usually didn't share because it wasn't anyone's damn business.

Savage smiled at Bowie, trying to deflect his question with one of his own. "Want to have a couple beers with me?" Savage knew he was pushing his luck with the younger guy, but he didn't give a shit. He was hot, tired and Bowie turned him the fuck on. It was time to knock off and if Savage could convince him to have a couple beers, then he might be able to talk Bowie into coming home with him for the night. If he was reading the signals correctly, his new friend was interested but he had been wrong in the past—so who knew.

"You asking me out, Savage?" Bowie questioned. Now it was Savage's turn to waiver in his answer and he suddenly worried that he had misread the chemistry that hummed through the air between the two of them.

Savage shrugged, "Maybe I am," he said, not really answering Bowie's question. The guy was as stoic as they came and Savage was trying to read him, but he wasn't having any luck.

"Listen, if I misread the situation, then just forget I asked," Savage grumbled. He picked up the last part of his rocket that landed a few hundred feet away from where he had parked and by the time he turned around and headed back to his pick-up truck, he found Bowie leaning up against the passenger side door, his hands shoved deep into his pockets.

"I'm in," Bowie said, flashing him a wolfish grin.

"Sounds good," Savage said. He was trying for nonchalant but his tone sounded anything but. It had been a damn long time since he met a man who made his cock pay attention, but Bowie did that for him. Savage needed to get himself under control or he'd blow his whole cool guy routine. Hell, he was far from being cool, but Bowie seemed interested and he wasn't about to do anything to fuck that up.

"You have someplace in mind?" Bowie asked, helping Savage shove the last of his equipment into the back of his pickup. "I mean, do you have a place you usually go to, you know, for a few beers?"

Savage liked the way Bowie seemed just as flustered about their situation as he was. He found it kind of cute the way the guy was floundering for words. He could have helped him out but giving him a hard time felt like the better option and would be a lot more fun.

"You mean, like a gay bar?" Savage asked. He knew he was adding fuel to the fire but he didn't care. Bowie turned an adorable shade of red that ran down his sexy neck and had Savage wanting to see just how far down his blush went.

"Well, I mean—sure. Or any bar, for that matter. It doesn't matter to me," Bowie stuttered.

Savage reached out and put his hand on Bowie's arm. "I'm

just messing with you," he said. "I don't know of too many gay bars in Huntsville. I usually just go to my own bar, but I don't really advertise that I'm gay and I don't feel like answering questions tonight. You mind just going to the Voodoo Lounge? It's a bit yuppie but I think we can blend in with the regular crowd. Plus, they've got great live music a few nights of the week."

"Wait—you have a bar?" Bowie asked.

Savage smiled and nodded, "Yep—the bar's called Savage Hell. It's also where my motorcycle club meets. We're a part of the Royal Bastards, which is a nationwide MC, but my little chapter calls themselves Savage Hell, after the bar. I try to keep my personal and private lives separate."

"Meaning you haven't shared that you're gay with your club," Bowie guessed.

Savage wasn't sure what to say to Bowie's assessment. On the one hand, he felt the need to set him straight and on the other, he wanted to tell him it wasn't anyone's business who he was having sex with. From the way his body was responding to Bowie, he hoped to have sex with him before the end of the night.

"Listen," Savage said. "I learned a long time ago that who I'm fucking is no one's business. I like you, Bowie but if you're not interested, tell me now if I'm wasting my time."

"I was just talking, man," Bowie said.

Savage sighed, "Yeah—I'm just on edge lately with these damn tests needing to be done yesterday and I'm being an ass. Sorry," he offered. "And to answer your question—I haven't told my club that I'm bi." Hell, he hadn't told many people about that part of his life. Savage was careful not to bring any of the men or women he slept with home to meet Chloe. He didn't want to expose his daughter to his unstable dating life and that was exactly what it was—chaotic.

He hadn't been much of a serial dater, usually not making it past one night with a person. It was easier that way. He didn't have to make any promises to anyone and he didn't expect anything in return. The one time he broke his no dating rule, he ended up running away like a fucking coward when messy feelings got in the way.

"So we doing this?" Savage asked. He started for the driver's side of his pick-up, not waiting to see if Bowie was going to join him or not.

"I get it," Bowie said. "I don't share that part of my life easily. I haven't even come out to my family yet." Bowie slipped into the passenger side of the cab of the truck and pulled his seatbelt on, clicking it in place.

"What about your truck?" Savage asked, nodding to where Bowie's vehicle sat, just down the road.

"I'll get it tomorrow when I'm back on duty. That is if you don't mind giving me a lift back to my place later." Bowie seemed to assume Savage would just agree and honestly, he didn't mind. If he was Bowie's ride for the night, there was a better chance they'd end up in Bowie's bed for a little while. Savage never left Chloe overnight, but he had a sitter with her and he knew that she'd agree to a few extra hours if he paid double.

"Sure," Savage said. "No problem."

"Thanks," Bowie said. "I have to admit, I could use a night out. It's been a shit show around base and I could use the break."

"Yeah, I heard about the cut-backs and I guess being down so many people makes for more work for the ones who are left." Savage knew some other guys on base from his club and they were all complaining about the changes to the budget and having to take on more hours for the same pay. His MC was made up of mostly military guys, both active and retired. But, his guys came from all walks of life—he even had a few one-percenters who he was happy to help get their lives straightened out. He liked helping his guys and even took a few of them under his wing, as a sort of personal project.

"Yep, it sucks. But, what am I gonna do? Uncle Sam owns me and I go where he tells me," Bowie said.

"Where are you originally from?" Savage asked. He usually didn't get too chatty with his "dates" but there was something about Bowie that made him want to know more about the guy.

"Texas," Bowie said.

"You get homesick?" Savage questioned.

"Naw," Bowie admitted. "Like I said, I still haven't come out to my family and keeping a secret like that weighs on a person. It's easier being away from home and not having to worry about watching my back or saying the wrong thing."

"I get that," Savage said. "I haven't exactly been forthcoming about my sexuality with my friends or family either." He had a few close buddies in his club that knew the truth and he trusted them not only with his secret but with his life.

"I'd like to blame my military background for all the secrecy, but that really isn't an issue anymore," Bowie said.

"Yeah, that wasn't the case when I enlisted." Savage had served under the, "Don't ask, don't tell," era and he had to admit, it had its pros and cons. Not having people diving too deep into his personal life was always a plus. He valued his privacy over everything else.

"You originally from Huntsville?" Bowie asked.

"Yeah," Savage said. "My family was from here, but they're all gone now. Well, everyone except Chloe and me." Savage mentally kicked himself for talking about his daughter. It wasn't something he did with complete strangers and he was starting to worry that asking Bowie out might have been a bad choice. Sure, the guy was the sexiest man he had seen in a damn long time but he was completely blowing his rules out the fucking window with Bowie and that usually didn't end well for him.

"Who's Chloe?" Bowie asked as if he was able to read Savage's mind.

"My kid," Savage admitted.

"You have a daughter?" Bowie asked.

"She's six and I adopted her when she was a baby. Chloe is my sister's kid and when she and her husband died in a car accident, I took Chloe in."

"Wow," Bowie breathed. "I'm sorry about your sister and brother-in-law. But, Chloe is lucky to have you, man."

Savage shrugged, "Thanks. And, I'm the lucky one. She came into my life when I was in a dark place and she gave me a purpose. She's a great kid."

"That makes sense," Bowie said. "She seems to have a pretty awesome dad."

BOWIE

Bowie wasn't sure how the hell he had ended up in the sexy stranger's pick-up agreeing to go for a few beers with him. He had been watching Savage for weeks now, not that he'd ever admit to it. Bowie had always been attracted to older men and Savage was his type, right down to his salt and pepper beard that made him want to give it a tug.

It had been a damn long time since he found anyone interesting enough to go out for a few beers with. When Savage first asked him out, he wasn't sure he had heard him correctly. He usually had a pretty good idea when a guy or woman, for that matter, was interested in him. But, Savage didn't give him anything to go by. It was hard to get a read on the guy and that made Bowie want him even more. He always did like a challenge.

Honestly, dating men was kind of new to him. He wasn't lying when he told Savage that he hadn't come out to his family yet. It was one of the reasons why he jumped at the chance to be transferred to Huntsville from Texas when the opportunity arose. He hated that he was taking the coward's way out, but that was easier than admitting that he was bi. He was even beginning to avoid his weekly calls home to his parents because he got sick of dodging their questions about if he had someone special in his life. Even if he had, he wouldn't be able to admit it because that would mean telling his parents who he was.

"You're awfully quiet," Savage said. "You having second thoughts?"

"About beer—never," Bowie teased. Savage shot him a smirk that told him he wasn't buying him using humor to hide from the question.

"You always a smart ass?" Savage asked.

"Most of the time," Bowie admitted. "I use humor to mask what I'm really feeling. My therapist says it's a way for me to hide my true self because I'm afraid that if people get to really know me, they won't like who I am." Bowie looked at Savage and almost made it through without busting up laughing. Savage looked about ready to pull to the side of the road and kick Bowie's ass out of his pick-up.

"Really, man," Savage grumbled. "I'm not sure if you're kidding or not." He shook his head at Bowie and smiled.

"Your face, man," Bowie said between fits of laughter.

"Yeah, yeah. Laugh it up," Savage griped. "Was any of that true?" The sad fact was it was all true but Bowie wouldn't admit that to Savage on what could potentially be their first date.

"Naw," Bowie lied. "I just like yanking people's chains." Savage looked at him as if he was trying to decide if he wanted to believe him or not. He seemed like a smart guy and if he was telling the truth earlier, a literal rocket scientist. Bowie worried that Savage would be able to see right through his facade and that scared the hell out of him.

"I mean, I've been to a therapist, but that was to work a few things out after I got back from active duty," Bowie admitted. Giving the guy some truth might throw him off the scent. It would be best to get through the night together without Savage finding out just how messed up he really was. That was another one of his secrets he didn't share with anyone—well, besides his therapist.

"Yeah—happens to the best of us. The Air Force shoved my ass into therapy after I got shot down, not that it helped much." Bowie knew just how a tragedy like that could affect a guy. He watched his best friend die after their Humvee was attacked. It should have been him who was lying on the side of the road, bleeding out but instead, it was his best friend, Drew.

They pulled into one of Huntsville's dive bars famous for its customers being a little on the shady side. It was a perfect spot for two guys who didn't want to be seen out together, to grab a few beers. No one got into anyone else's business in places like the Voodoo Lounge and that was just the way they both seemed to want it. He knew that score—Savage didn't look like the type of guy who did long- term relationships and that was fine with Bowie. He wasn't sure where he'd be tomorrow and settling down with someone like Savage seemed like a pipe dream. He never let himself imagine his life with a man. Hell, he never imagined settling down with anyone, if he was being completely honest.

Savage parked his truck and cut the engine. "Listen, man," he sighed, "if you changed your mind about all of this, I'd get it."

Bowie smiled at Savage and reached across the center console to take his hand. "You keep saying that, Savage. But, I haven't changed my mind—about the beer or you. I'd like to hang out with you tonight, no pressure and no strings. You up for that?" Savage nodded and if Bowie wasn't mistaken, he could have sworn the big guy was blushing.

"I'd like that," he said. Savage grabbed his baseball cap from the back seat and covered his bald head, running his hand down his beard and Bowie couldn't seem to take his eyes off the guy. He was hot as fuck and Bowie was mesmerized by his every movement. He had been for weeks, following him around, watching him on base. Savage was big but carried himself with confidence and grace. He had a persona that screamed alpha and that alone turned Bowie completely the fuck on. He liked older men because the few he had been with usually insisted on being in charge in the bedroom. He wondered if Savage would be just as demanding and the thought sent a shiver down his body.

"You good?" Savage asked. Bowie shook his head and smiled.

"No, but it's nothing a few beers won't fix," Bowie lied. He had a feeling it would take more than alcohol to right what had been bothering him. In fact, Bowie had a sneaky feeling it would take at least a night of taking orders from the sexy man sitting next to him to start feeling like himself again.

SAVAGE

Savage felt about ready to turn back around and leave just as soon as he saw his ex sitting at the bar with her girlfriends. Apparently, one of them was about to get hitched and Dallas was there to help her celebrate. At least, that was what he had gathered from the group of rowdy women.

"Shit," he grumbled and sat down next to Bowie. He looked down at the end of the bar to where Dallas mean-mugged him and had the nerve to laugh.

"I'd say 'shit' doesn't even begin to cover it judging from the way that blonde is scowling at you, man. What did you do?" Bowie asked. That really was a loaded question. It was more like what he didn't do that was the problem. She was the only woman that Savage dated more than just a few times. Hell, she was the only person he had any kind of relationship within his entire adult life. And, he fucked it completely up with her. He ghosted Dallas when he realized he wasn't going to be able to commit to her. She'd never be enough for him and how did he admit something like that to her? It was easier to just walk away from her and hope that Dallas would just forget about him. Her angry scowl told him that hadn't happened yet.

"We dated," Savage admitted. "About a year ago."

"Wow," Bowie whistled under his breath. "So, whatever you did to that woman must have been big, if she hasn't forgiven you in a year."

"I didn't ask for forgiveness," Savage growled. "And, I'm not looking for it now."

"Well, I didn't have you pegged as the dating type," Bowie said. Savage held up two fingers to the bartender, signaling that he wanted a couple beers. The bar really didn't offer much in the way of choices and he was one of the regulars, on nights after he had a rough day at work and didn't want to deal with his MC brothers asking him a million questions. At the Voodoo Lounge, he could just be himself and no one really bothered him.

The bartender brought them their beers and a bowl of pretzels that looked like they had been set out for a few weeks. "Hey, Savage," the bartender said.

"Mike." Savage nodded. "Start me a tab," he ordered.

"Sure thing," Mike agreed and nodded to Bowie.

"You new here?" he asked.

"Yeah," Bowie said. "New to the area, really. I'm at Redstone Arsenal." Mike grunted and Bowie smiled.

"Well, women around these parts seem to burst into flames around guys in uniform. Just watch yourself with the piranhas at the end of the bar. One of the chicks is getting married but they seem to be out for a good time. Just fair warning; unless you're looking for something like that." Mike looked between Bowie and Savage as if trying to access what was going on between the two of them and Savage growled.

"Thanks, Mike," he barked, all but dismissing the guy. Bowie laughed again and he wondered what was so funny but he had a feeling he wouldn't like Bowie's answer. So, he didn't bother asking.

"Are you always so grumbly?" Bowie accused.

"No," Savage quickly defended, shooting him a look that probably told him he was lying. Bowie held up his hands as if in defense.

"Okay, man," he said. "No need to bite my head off. If you want to go someplace else, we can. Hell, we can go back to my apartment. I have beer there." Bowie shot him a wolfish grin, making Savage smile.

"I'm good here," Savage lied. He could feel Dallas' eyes boring into the back of his head and he wasn't sure what the hell to do about her.

"Liar," Bowie challenged. "That sexy blonde has you squirming in your seat. It's hot, really—the thought of you with her. I just don't want to cause any trouble. Does she know?"

"Know what?" Savage asked, playing dumb.

Bowie sighed. "Does she know that you date guys?" he whispered.

"No," Savage breathed. He sucked down half his beer and shot a look across the bar to where Dallas was still giving him the stink-eye.

"You ghost her or something?" Bowie teased and Savaged winced. "Fuck, man," Bowie spat. "You didn't fucking ghost that hot woman sitting at the end of the bar?"

"I did and can you keep it down, man?" Savage said.

"I'm pretty sure she can't hear me over this God awful honky-tonk music and the ruckus her girlfriends are making. Why did you do it?" Bowie asked.

"Because she would never be enough for me," Savage

admitted. It was the truest thing he had said to Bowie and he worried that made him sound like an ass. "We had been on a few dates and I really liked her, but then I realized that if I dated her—you know, just her—I'd be denying half of myself. You know what I mean?"

Bowie nodded like he understood exactly what Savage was talking about and he realized that he had just assumed the guy was gay.

"You like women too?" Savage asked.

"Yep," Bowie admitted." In fact, I haven't been with many men. It was easier to deny that part of who I was while I was living so close to home. I didn't start exploring that side of my sexuality until I was stationed here. I had been on a few dates with men, but not a lot. So, I do get what you're talking about, man."

Savage sat back in his barstool and waved the bartender back over. "We'll take two more and buy the ladies at the end of the bar another round on me," he said. Mike nodded and walked back down to where the loud group of women sat and when he announced that Savage wanted to buy them a round of drinks, they all squealed and cheered. Well, everyone except Dallas. She shot him a look that could stop most men dead in their tracks, but he wasn't most men.

Dallas stood from her stool and started toward them and Bowie cursed. "Um, I'm pretty sure the shit is about to hit the fucking fan now, Savage," he said. Savage had a bad feeling that Bowie was right.

He held his breath, second-guessing every decision he had made that day, right down to asking Bowie out and buying Dallas' friends a round of drinks. Yep, he was thoroughly fucked and all he wanted to do was get the hell out of there. Savage stood and threw down a hundred dollar bill, knowing that would cover his tab, and smiled at Bowie.

"That offer to get a beer at your place still stand?" Savage asked.

Bowie smiled and nodded. "Sure," he said. "But, for the record, you're being a chicken." He looked across the bar to where Dallas was making her way across the crowded dance floor and sighed. Bowie was right but he didn't give a fuck. Better to leave as a chicken then face his ex's wrath.

"Yep," he breathed. "Ready?" He held out his hand for Bowie, knowing he might be sending not only Dallas but everyone who was currently watching the exchange between them, a clear sign that the two of them were together.

Bowie took his hand and they made their way to the front of the bar. Just as Savage stepped out of the doorway and into the night, he looked back to find Dallas watching him; frozen to her spot with her mouth gaping wide open. Yeah, she had gotten the message, loud and clear—he was leaving the bar with Bowie and there would be no back-tracking now. There would be nothing he could do to erase the hatred and pain that he saw in her beautiful eyes.

DALLAS

Dallas St. James just about fell off her damn barstool when Savage walked into The Voodoo Lounge with the handsome guy in fatigues. The two made quite a pair and she wasn't the only female in the bar to notice them. Every woman in her group seemed to sit up and take notice of the new conquests as soon as they walked in, even the bride-to-be.

She thought she'd never see Savage again and that was just fine with her. They had dated for about a month and then nothing—he seemed to vanish off the face of the earth. It was her fault really. She never pushed to know more about him than his first name and the fact that he used to be in the Air Force. He had mentioned that he was a scientist, but Dallas worried that if she pushed for him to tell her more, he'd bolt. It was ironic, really. He ended up changing her life forever and then ghosting her, never to be heard from again —or so she thought.

Dallas was determined to steer clear of Savage and whoever the guy was that came into the bar with him, but then he went too far and bought the bridal party a round of drinks. Was he trying to get her attention? If he was, it worked. By the time she got her nerve up, Savage and the guy got up to leave but what she saw next—it couldn't have been right. The bar was crowded and she had to have seen the whole thing wrong because if she wasn't mistaken, they were holding hands when they left the bar.

She tried to rejoin her girlfriends, but she just wasn't in the mood to party after seeing Savage. He dredged up everything she had worked so hard to suppress—her anger, her fears and damn it, even her desires. How could she still want him like she did after the hell he'd put her through over the past year since he left her without a word? Sure, Savage didn't make her any pretty promises. She thought she meant more to him than just a fuck, but she was wrong. She had not only misjudged him but so many other things too.

Dallas bowed out of the rest of the night, not really in the mood for the strip club the girls were heading to next. All she could think about was getting back to her little apartment and shutting the world out until she could think straight again. Savage always seemed to have that effect on her—made her thoughts a little cloudy. Seeing him tonight just reminded her of the crazy, lust- filled month that they spent together and she needed to put those thoughts and images out of her head. There would be no more remembering the man who controlled her body, mind, and soul. Savage threw her away and that was going to be the painful reminder she took home with her tonight. He didn't want her and she'd do well to remember that.

Dallas climbed the two floors to her apartment and unlocked the door, letting herself in. "Hello," she whispered.

"Hey—did you have fun?" Her friend Eden poked her head around the corner and smiled. "I'm assuming that since you are home so early that my answer is no, but I thought I'd be polite and ask."

Dallas made a face and Eden softly cursed. "You saw him, didn't you? She asked. Her friend always was able to pick up things.

"How the hell did you figure that out?" Dallas grumbled.

"You make a face anytime his name is brought up. Listen, I've never met the guy, but you're going to have to get over this anger you're harboring towards him. If not for yourself then for Greer," Eden said.

Dallas sighed and nodded. Her friend was right—she owed it to both herself and her daughter to stop hating the man who had given her the greatest gift she ever had.

"I ran into him tonight at The Voodoo Lounge," Dallas admitted.

"Well, shit. That's not good. Did you talk to him?" Eden asked. Dallas could hear the question her friend was really asking her.

"Just go ahead and ask," Dallas said.

"Did you tell him about Greer?" Eden dramatically whispered.

Dallas shook her head. "No. I didn't even get the chance to talk to him. He was sitting across the bar with some really good looking guy and by the time I tried to make it across the crowded dance floor, they bolted."

"Good," Eden said. "You don't owe him anything, Dallas. He used you and left you pregnant and alone. Hell, you didn't even know if that fucker was alive or dead. Telling him about Greer would be a huge mistake." Dallas wondered if her friend was right. For months after Savage cut off contact with her, she worried that he had been in some horrific accident and was hurt or worse—dead. It was silly really but believing some made up tragic story was so much easier than knowing the truth. He just walked away from her and that realization stung like a son-of-a-bitch. Eden was right about one thing—Savage used her and didn't even have the common decency to tell her it was over. He was a coward and he showed his true colors tonight when he ran out of that bar again.

"Maybe you're right," Dallas said with a shrug.

"No maybe about it, girl. You've proven that you don't need his damn help with Greer. You're an awesome mom and your daughter will get everything she needs from you and well—me, her fabulous auntie."

Dallas giggled, "Thanks, fabulous auntie," she teased. "I needed to hear that tonight. It was just so strange, you know?"

"You mean seeing him again?" Eden asked.

"No—the way he left out of that bar. First, he took off like his pants were on fire and then, I could have sworn that he was holding hands with the hot guy he was with."

"What?" Eden questioned. "As in—they were there together, on a date?"

"Yeah, but that's crazy, right?" Dallas asked. Maybe she hadn't seen them correctly or she had just misread the situation.

"Well, that would explain why he ghosted you," Eden offered. "Maybe he realized he liked being with guys," she teased.

"Are you implying that I turned him gay?" Dallas mocked upset and Eden giggled.

"That is one explanation," Eden joked, but Dallas found the whole topic less funny than her friend seemed to. Dallas had more at stake in all of this—she had more to lose and there would be no way she'd take chances with her daughter's happiness, not even for the sexiest man she had ever known. When Savage walked away from her, he didn't realize he was also leaving behind a little piece of himself that would remind Dallas, every day, of the time they had spent together. Her three-month-old daughter, Greer, was the spitting image of her father and the reason why she needed to work through her anger towards Savage. She owed her daughter at least that much.

BOWIE

Bowie grabbed two beers from his fridge and found Savage sitting on his little sofa, brooding. God, the guy was sexy as fuck when he was angry and for some reason, the hot blonde at the bar seemed to make Savage madder than hell.

"Here," Bowie said, pushing the beer at him. "I think you might need this."

"Thanks," Savage said, taking the bottle from him.

"Want to tell me about her?" Bowie asked. Really, the last thing he wanted to do with Savage was talk about the woman at the bar. He wasn't really jealous that Savage had dated her, but he wished he could get under the big guy's skin as much as the blonde seemed to.

"No," Savage lied. "Dallas and I went on a few dates and that's it, really."

"Liar," Bowie accused. He knew there had to be more to the story than what Savage was telling him. The way she looked at Savage with so much contempt, he knew that Savage was leaving out a vital part.

"So, you ghosted her and then what?" Bowie pushed. Savage growled and set his beer down.

"I didn't come here to talk about my ex or my past fuck-ups. I came here to hopefully have a few beers and get to know you," Savage said.

"I'm calling bullshit on that one too," Bowie said. He set his beer next to Savage's and slid closer to him on the sofa. "You didn't come here to get to know me," he challenged. "You came here for this," he said. Bowie pulled Savage against his body and sealed his mouth over his, using his surprised gasp to gain entry with his tongue. By the time Bowie broke their kiss, they were both panting for air and their raw need seemed to hum through the room.

"Fuck," Savage growled. "Do that again," he ordered. Bowie was right—Savage was bossy and that was just the way he liked his guys. Bowie did exactly as ordered, straddling Savage's big lap and covering his body with his own. Bowie could feel Savage's heart racing under his t-shirt and it was doing all kinds of crazy things to his libido. Knowing that Savage was just as turned on by the whole scene as he was made him hard.

"You feel so fucking good," Bowie whispered against his lips. He ground his own cock against Savage's letting him feel every inch of his arousal. Bowie fucked his lips just the way he wanted to fuck Savage's ass and he just hoped to God that was the way their evening together was going to end. He needed to find his release and he hoped that Savage would agree to let him do it in his sexy as sin ass.

"Bed," Savage gasped between kisses. "Naked," he ordered.

Bowie smiled down at him and nodded. "I want in your ass," he admitted.

"Fine," Savage barked. "But first, you're going to give me a blow job and get me off." Bowie loved that Savage was calling the shots. The thought of wrapping his lips around Savage's dick made him nearly come in his damn pants.

"Yes," he hissed. He stood from Savage's lap and pulled him up from the sofa, leading the way back through his tiny apartment to his bedroom. Bowie pushed Savage back against his bed, liking the way he fell onto the mattress, accepting whatever fate Bowie had planned for him. He unbuckled Savage's jeans and pulled them down his thick thighs.

"No underwear?" Bowie asked. He made a mock tsking noise and Savage laughed.

"I don't own underwear," Savage said.

"Fuck, that's hot," Bowie groaned. He palmed Savage's impressive erection and knelt over him, sucking him completely into his mouth. When Savage shoved in further, to the back of his throat, Bowie swallowed around his cock, causing him to moan out his name.

"You keep doing that and I won't last long, Babe," Savage growled. Hearing the little term of endearment made Bowie's heart do a flip-flop in his chest. He needed to keep his head in the damn game and remember that wasn't what this was between the two of them. This was just a fuck to Savage and Bowie needed to play the game. Savage had already made it loud and clear that he wasn't looking for anything more. The last thing Bowie wanted was to end up the jilted ex giving him the stink-eye across a crowded bar. It seemed that Savage already had a not so secret ex-lover that was handling that role quite well.

Savage took over, pumping his cock in and out of Bowie's willing mouth, taking exactly what he needed from him. He knew Savage was close and when he hoarsely cried out

Bowie's name and came down his throat, Bowie swallowed all of him and licked him clean.

"God, Babe," Savage whispered. He was trying to catch his breath and Bowie smiled down at him, damn proud of what he had just given Savage.

"Wait here," Bowie ordered. He ran to his bathroom and grabbed the lube and a condom. He needed in Savage's ass, as promised, or he was going to burst.

"Up," Bowie ordered. Savage seemed just as willing to take direction, doing as Bowie had ordered. He bent over Bowie's bed and let him rub lube in his ass. Bowie let his hand trail down to Savage's balls and gently caressed them, feeling his cock spring to life again.

"You're going to feel so good, Savage," he crooned. He put the condom on and lubed up his cock and when he lined himself up to take Savage's ass, his guy pushed back against him, taking him all in just one thrust.

"Shit, man," Bowie shouted. "Fuck, you're going to have to give me a minute." Savage felt so fucking good, he knew he wasn't going to last long. Bowie thrust in and out of Savage's body, loving the way he ruthlessly pushed back into him with every thrust as if challenging him to be rougher than he already was. Savage was a beast and Bowie's only thought was to tame him. When he came, he shouted Savage's name and collapsed on top of him, pushing Savage face-first into the mattress.

"That was—" Bowie didn't get to finish his thought before Savage was rolling out from underneath him to stand.

"Great," he finished for Bowie. "But, I have to get going."

"Going?" Bowie questioned. "You alright, Savage?" He asked. He knew Savage was running scared but he wasn't about to hold the guy up from making his hasty retreat. If

Savage wanted to fuck him and then run off, that was on him.

"Yep," Savage lied.

"Wow," Bowie whispered. "You really don't do the whole dating thing at all, do you?" Savage pulled on his pants and tugged his shirt over his head. He was getting dressed so fast, he looked like a blur of arms and legs. It was almost comical but Bowie wasn't in the mood to find anything funny. Instead of amused, he was feeling used and a little hurt.

"I have a kid—remember? I need to get home before the babysitter's time is up and I promised Chloe I'd be home in time to tuck her in."

"Okay," Bowie said. He couldn't fault the guy for wanting to get home to see his kid before she went to bed. "Will I see you again?" God, he sounded like a lovesick schoolgirl and he wanted to stop talking but that was proving impossible.

"I mean—only if you want to see me again. I know what this was, Savage and if you are just a one night kind of guy, then I get it." Bowie couldn't seem to stop the verbal diarrhea that was running out of his mouth. And, Savage had the nerve to laugh at him. Bowie wanted to crawl under the bed and stay there until Savage was gone, but he said what he said and taking it all back now was impossible.

"Geeze Bowie. Take a breath, man," Savage teased. "Besides seeing you around the arsenal, I'd like you to come over to my house for dinner this Friday if you are free. Chloe has a sleepover at a friend's house and you can even spend the night if you want."

Bowie whistled, "Well, I didn't see that one coming," he teased. Savage gave him a sexy smirk and shrugged.

"Me either, really. Listen, Bowie—I don't get all mushy and sentimental. I don't do flowery, romantic gestures; that's just not me. If you need all that shit, then this might not work," Savage said, motioning between them.

"No, I'm good with no romantic shit. I was just not expecting a second date is all." Bowie stood and made his way to the bathroom to discard the condom and pulled on a pair of gym shorts. He found Savage standing by his front door as if he had a meter running on an Uber.

"So, we on for Friday?" Savage asked. Bowie nodded and brushed past Savage to open the front door. Savage grabbed his arm and pulled him back against his body. "Was that a yes?" Savage questioned.

Bowie smiled at him, "Yes," he agreed. "I'll see you Friday. Just text me your address and I'll be off at about five. I'll need to grab a quick shower and then I can be over to your place around six if that works. I'll bring the beer," he offered.

"Sounds good," Savage said. He kissed Bowie and then left, leaving him to wonder what the hell had just happened. The man he'd been watching for weeks now not only ended up in his bed but was agreeing to see him again. Bowie always did like surprises and Savage was turning into quite the surprise first date, considering it was leading to a second one and he didn't see that one coming at all.

SAVAGE

What the fuck was wrong with him? He had just spent the evening with a damn near perfect guy and here all Savage could think about was the sexy little blonde who gave him the evil eye all night long. He went and acted like a complete ass to Bowie; running out of his fucking apartment as fast as humanly possible to drive all the way back to The Voodoo Lounge to see if Dallas was still there.

Yep, he was a complete asshole and if Bowie found out about why he had hightailed it out of his place so fast, he'd probably never speak to him again and Savage wouldn't blame him. If the situation was reversed, he'd feel the same way. He drove straight to the bar, sending his sitter a quick text that he was going to be a little later than usual. He offered to pay her double and she agreed to stay an extra hour with Chloe. He was going to miss saying goodnight to his little princess and tucking her into bed as promised, and that pissed him off. He was mad at himself but there was no way around it. He needed to find Dallas and explain to her what happened. He needed to apologize and beyond that, he was secretly hoping she'd give him another fucking chance. After the night he had with Bowie and the mind-blowing orgasm he had, the only thing he could think about was putting Dallas between the two of them.

The problem was getting Bowie to agree to his crazy idea. Hell, the problem would be getting Dallas to give him five minutes of her time and not rip his fucking heart out of his chest. He'd deserve it too, but that wouldn't stop him from trying. He parked in front of the bar and looked around the lot as if expecting to find her standing there waiting for him. Instead, he found the place had pretty much emptied out and his heart sank.

Savage walked into the bar, pretending to be cool and collected although he felt anything but. "Hey, Savage," the bartender called. "You forget something?" He wanted to tell Mike that he had forgotten his damn rules because apparently, that was true. His rules were in place for a reason and not getting too involved with anyone seemed like a damn good rule right about now. But here he was, wanting to get into a messy situation with not one but two people and that drove him just about fucking nuts.

"No," Savage said, doing a quick surveillance of the bar. When he spied the bride-to-be from earlier, he wasn't sure if he felt relief or panic. He needed to man-up and ask her where Dallas was. That was why he drove back across town and left a warm bed with a sexy as fuck, willing man, wasn't it?

"Excuse me," Savage yelled over the bad honky-tonk music. The woman turned and eyed him and then smiled as if she recognized him.

"Hey—it's you," she slurred.

"Yeah," Savage said. "Um, your friend that was here,

earlier—Dallas," he started. The bride-to-be threw her body up against his and practically knocked him over.

"You're the nice guy who bought us all drinks," she stammered. Apparently, he wasn't the only person buying the bridal party drinks, judging by how drunk the woman was.

"Um, sure," he agreed. "Listen, the woman who was here earlier, Dallas," he tried again.

"Have you ever been to Texas?" She interrupted again.

"Yes," he said. "Damn it, will you just listen to me for a second?" The woman looked as if he had slapped her and he felt like a complete ass. "I'm sorry," he said. "I shouldn't have yelled, but I'm looking for Dallas. It's kind of important."

"She had to go home," the woman slurred. "Her babysitter called because the baby won't stop crying."

"Baby?" he asked. Savage had no clue Dallas had a kid.

"Yeah—she just had a kid a few months back and that bitch has the nerve to look as good as she did tonight. I bet she doesn't even have stretch marks."

"A few months?" Savage questioned. He was trying to do some quick math in his head and it was starting to all add up. "Is Dallas with the baby's father?" Savage asked. He was afraid that he already knew the answer, but he still asked.

"No," the woman confirmed. "Dallas is a single mom— poor thing." She made an effort to pout and it was almost comical. At least it would have been funny if Savage wasn't just hearing for the first time of the possibility that he was a father, from some drunk chick in a dive bar. Not exactly how he saw this whole night ending. Hell, nothing about today had gone as planned and he worried he was going to open a can of worms that might be better off left closed. The problem was—if Dallas had his kid and didn't tell him, he'd want to know. Hell, he'd want to be a part of his kid's life, no matter how badly the mom hated him and if Dallas was keeping his baby from him then he had a feeling she hated him a whole fucking lot.

"Thanks," Savage said. "And good luck with the wedding." He turned to leave, trying to remember where Dallas lived. It had been about a year since he was at her place but he was pretty sure he knew the route. There was no fucking way he was going to ignore the possibility that she had his kid and waiting until tomorrow wasn't an option either. He was going to find Dallas' apartment and then he was going to stop being a fucking chicken and find out what the hell was going on. If he had a kid out there, he was going to be a part of his or her life or at least he'd fight like hell to be.

SAVAGE DROVE AROUND HUNTSVILLE, trying to find the road that led back to Dallas' apartment complex and after about an hour of driving in circles, he was about ready to give up. That was when he spotted the sign to her complex and headed to the back of the development, knowing she was in the last building. He parked his pick-up and took a deep breath, trying to steady his nerves. He remembered the way her blue eyes looked straight through him tonight and how angry she seemed to be with him. She had every right to be—he had cut off all communication with her and that was a shitty thing to do. But, there had to be some way for her to reach him, especially if she was pregnant with his baby. He tried to think back to what he had told her about himself. Savage cursed when he realized that he probably hadn't even told her his full name. How was she supposed to track him down if she knew close to nothing about him?

He needed facts—the first being if the baby was his or not. Hell, first he needed to find out if there was a baby. He couldn't go off half-cocked making assumptions based on the ramblings of a drunk bride-to-be. He'd have to figure out the rest of this mess from there.

He found Dallas' apartment and banged on her front door, not really caring what time it was. He had to pound on the door three more times before a very groggy, sexy, and pissed-off Dallas answered the door wearing not much more than a snug t-shirt and a scowl.

"If you wake my kid," she whispered. Dallas didn't even have the door fully opened when she seemed to realize who was on the other side, she quickly tried to close it. Savage stuck his boot in the door jam, effectively stopping her from slamming it in his face.

"You can't just show up at my home and push your way in, Savage," she shouted.

"I thought we were being quiet, so we don't wake the kid," he growled. Dallas stopped trying to fight him and dropped her arms to her side. "I think we need to talk, Dallas," he said.

Dallas barked out her laugh and he knew from just that sound alone that she was going to give him a fight. "So, now you want to talk to me, Savage? You disappeared from my life and just show up, out of the blue, and I'm supposed to what—put on a pot of tea and invite you into my home to catch up?"

"Well, if we could make it that easy, then sure," Savage teased.

"You ghosted me," Dallas accused. A baby started crying and Dallas strung together an impressive strand of curses that made Savage smile. She was always so inventive when it came to cursing. His favorite tonight was her calling him a cuntwaffle, cock-sucking, son of a whore as she stepped to the side and ushered him into her apartment to shut her door behind him.

He watched as she disappeared down the small hallway that he knew led back to two bedrooms. Her place was small but cozy and he had spent a few nights with her there when Chloe slept over at friends' houses.

Dallas came back a few minutes later, cradling a baby against her chest, trying to rock the screaming newborn back to sleep. "I really didn't need this tonight," she grouched. "I have an early morning meeting tomorrow and I just needed a few hours' sleep." Savage barely heard a word she was saying, fixated on the tiny person in her arms.

"Boy or girl?" Savage asked, not taking his eyes off the baby.

Dallas sighed. "Girl," she said. "Her name is Greer." She kissed the top of the baby's little head and Savage didn't hold back. He had a slew of questions he needed answers to and before he left her apartment tonight, Dallas was going to answer every one of them.

"Is she mine?" he asked. Savage didn't plan on starting with that one, right out of the gate, but he thought it was the most important one. If the baby wasn't his, he would have no right to ask the other questions that were running through his mind.

"Listen, I have to feed her and now isn't the time for this discussion," Dallas challenged.

"Shit," he said. "Yes or no, Dallas—is she mine?"

"Fine—" she spat. "She's yours."

"Well, fuck," he barked. All the questions that were so important a few seconds ago suddenly felt unnecessary. Only one seemed to stick in his head and he had to know. "You didn't think I had a right to know that I was going to be a father, Dallas?"

"Sure," she said. Dallas sat down on her sofa and pulled her shirt up to feed the baby. He watched, fascinated at how his daughter latched on to eat with a fury that made him want to laugh. Greer instantly stopped crying and settled down.

"Why didn't you tell me about her?" he almost whispered.

"You really didn't leave me that option, Savage," she said. He sat down next to her and gently rubbed the baby's fuzzy little head of dark hair. She was so tiny. When Chloe came to him, she was already six months old and he remembered thinking she was so small, he was afraid he'd break her. Greer was only half of Chloe's size though and the same thoughts ran through his mind.

"How old is she?" He asked.

"Almost three months," Dallas said. "I had no way of finding you, Savage. Hell, I don't even know your last name," she admitted. He winced at that truth. He hadn't shared much with her. They usually met out for dinner and then ended up back at her apartment. She didn't even know about Chloe. He was determined to keep Dallas at arm's length because the feelings he started having for her scared the fuck out of him. Every time he spent the night with her, he went home the next morning not able to concentrate on anything or anyone else. She was consuming his waking and sleeping thoughts and that's probably why he just cut her out of his life. It was easier than dealing with his feelings and all that messy relationship stuff he couldn't stop thinking about.

"Savage is my last name," he admitted. "My name is Logan Savage." Dallas nodded and pulled Greer free from her breast to burp her. His daughter let out a massive burp and then Dallas switched sides, to continue feeding the baby.

"I'm sorry," he whispered.

"The time for sorry has passed, Savage. I've had to deal with all this alone and you know what—I've done a damn good job of it. You came here to find out if the baby is yours? Well, now you know." Savage knew she was dismissing him, but he didn't give a shit. He'd never be able to leave and pretend he didn't have a kid out there. Greer was his daughter and he wanted to be a part of her life, even if that meant groveling to Dallas for forgiveness, he'd do it.

"I get that you're pissed and you have every right to be, Honey. But, I want to be a part of her life," he said. Savage thought it best to leave out the part where he wanted to be a part of Dallas' life too.

"No," she said. "Not happening. What happens when you get bored with her and just ghost your own daughter. I'm betting you have no desire to be a dad, Savage and that's fine. I can be enough for our kid and she'll never have to live with the disappointment of you not showing up."

"Now you're just pissing me off, Dallas," he growled. "I know I didn't share much of who I am with you but I'm a damn good father. I have a six-year-old daughter and I'd never abandon my kid."

"You have a daughter?" Dallas asked as if she didn't believe a word he was telling her.

Savage nodded, "Yeah. She's my whole world and the reason why I never took you back to my house. I adopted her when she was six months old. She was my sister Cherry's kid. My sister was in an accident with her husband and they both died. Chloe was in the back seat and slept through the whole ordeal and came out completely unscathed. Well, unless you count being orphaned. Cherry named me as Chloe's next of kin, even though we hadn't spoken for years and well, I adopted her."

"Wow," Dallas said. "I think you just told me more about yourself in the last five minutes than you did in the month we were together," she said.

"I'd like the chance to know my daughter, Dallas," he said. "Please," he begged.

Dallas finished feeding Greer and burped her again. The baby settled down and fell back to sleep on Dallas' shoulder and Savage smiled at the way a little milk drool escaped her open mouth. She was beautiful.

"Why did you do it?" Dallas whispered. "Why didn't you face me to tell me we were done? Do you know what it did to me to be ghosted? It felt like I didn't matter as a person, Savage."

Hearing that made him feel like shit but he couldn't take back the past. "I'm an ass," he said, knowing that explanation wasn't enough. Savage brushed the sleeping infant's little cheek and smiled.

"What happened between us scared me," he admitted. Savage hated talking about his fucking feelings. He avoided it at all costs but knowing that he hurt Dallas made him feel like shit and he owed her an honest answer. "I never really dated before."

"I hardly call what we did dating," she said. "I mean, sure you took me to dinner most of the time but we ended up back here and well." Dallas looked down at the sleeping baby on her shoulder as if proving her point.

Savage smiled. "Yeah," he breathed. "Well, being with you was as close to dating as I've ever gotten." Dallas giggled and he feigned hurt. "Why are you laughing?"

"I mean, you're what in your forties, right?"

"I'm forty-five. Why?" he asked.

"You honestly expect me to believe that you have never dated anyone seriously before me? Come on, Savage." Dallas did have a point but he really didn't want to get into his issues with being bi. Savage always felt torn between two worlds, as if he didn't really belong in either. There would be no way around telling Dallas that he was into guys too—not now. It was the only way to explain why he took off on her the way he did.

"I'm bi," he said.

"As in bisexual?" Dallas asked.

"Yes," he confirmed. "I like guys too."

"I'm clear on what being bi means, Savage," she said. Dallas stood and put Greer in her bassinet and stood back to watch her squirming daughter. Savage remembered doing the same with Chloe when he first adopted her, holding his breath and praying she didn't wake back up. When Greer settled, Dallas let out her pent-up breath and Savage chuckled.

"They are a little nerve-wracking," he said. "I used to hold my breath and pray Chloe would go back to sleep too."

Dallas shook her head and smiled. "Greer isn't the best sleeper and I find myself doing a hell of a lot more praying than I ever have in my life. Usually, it's more like bargaining with God that if he lets me get some sleep, I'll be a better person. It's not a stretch, really. I am a nicer person when I'm rested." Savage chuckled and Dallas sat down next to him on the sofa and for the first time that night, she looked him in the eyes and all he could think about doing was pulling her onto his lap and kissing her the way he used to, but he didn't.

"That guy you were with tonight?" Dallas whispered.

"Yeah," he said, not letting her finish her question.

"Do you like guys better? Was that the issue with us not working out?" she asked.

"No—no preference," he lied. He had a preference but that would involve something Dallas might not be ready for. He wasn't sure she'd be up for a threesome and there was no way he'd chance ruining not just one person's life but two.

"Are you two together then?" She asked.

"That's not a yes or no question, really," he stalled. "Tonight was our first date," he admitted.

"God, that's awful," she said. "You're out on your first date with the guy and you run into me?" She started to giggle and by the time she finished, she was practically on top of him. When she realized how close they were, she sobered and cleared her throat.

"I'm not sure what to do about all of this," Savage whispered. "I mean—seeing you again and then finding out about Greer." A part of him wished he could go back to earlier that afternoon when all he had to worry about was a failed rocket test. But, taking it all back wasn't the answer. Meeting Bowie was something he wouldn't want to take back and finding out about his daughter was definitely not something he'd want to forget about. It just felt like life was moving at warp speed around him and he just needed the ride to slow down a little.

"What do we do now?" Dallas asked. "I don't suppose you can go back to forgetting about me and the fact that you have a daughter?"

"No," Savage breathed. "I can't. How about we take this one step at a time. I'd like to get to know Greer and introduce her to Chloe. She's always wanted a little brother or sister."

Dallas smiled. "I'd like for Greer to meet Chloe, but what about us? Can we call a truce and get along?" Savage wanted to tell her that he wanted to do more than call a fucking truce between the two of them, but he'd give her the words she needed—for now. Seeing her tonight just drove home those same damn feelings he felt for her a year ago when he acted like a fucking coward. But this time, instead of being afraid of all the emotions and feelings, he decided to try something new. This time, he was going to take some of his own advice and face his fears.

"How about this Friday night?" Dallas asked. "I'm working both jobs until then but that's my next night off."

"You work two jobs?" Savage asked.

"Yeah well, being an administrative assistant doesn't pay enough to cover the bills and with Greer," she paused to look over to where their daughter slept. "Well, babies aren't cheap. If you can do Friday, I think we can arrange for the girls to meet and then you and I can work a few things out."

Savage hated that he was going to have to cancel on Bowie but what choice did he have? He wouldn't walk away from his daughter and Dallas was right—they needed to work a few things out. Namely—the fact that he was going to help pay for his daughter and she was going to have to accept his help. But that would be a fight for another day.

"Friday works," he lied.

DALLAS

Dallas wasn't sure why she was such a nervous wreck. It was probably due to the fact that she was about to see the sexiest man she had ever known, who also happened to be her baby's father. She also had four very long days to play through all the scenarios and worry about having to see him again, which didn't help her already worn nerves.

Savage had given her his cell number before leaving earlier that week when he showed up at her apartment demanding to know if Greer was his. Friday morning, she texted him to ask if they were still on for their meeting that evening, and he texted back that they were and sent her an address. Dallas pulled up her map app on her cell and when she realized the place he wanted her to meet him was a bar, she almost called him back and told him to forget it. But, this wasn't about her. It was about her daughter and if dealing with Savage meant that Greer would have her dad in her life, it would be worth it.

So, instead of calling to cancel, she decided to call to

double-check the address that he sent her was correct. Of course, Savage answered on the very first ring, throwing her completely off her game.

"Hey," his sexy, gravelly voice answered.

"Um, hi," she squeaked.

"You good?" He asked.

"Of course," she lied. "I just wanted to make sure you sent me the correct address. The place you have me meeting you is a bar," she said.

Savage chuckled into the phone and her girl parts did a little happy dance. Savage was the last man she was with and Dallas was starting to realize that maybe that was a mistake. She needed to get laid—preferably soon.

"Yeah, it's my bar. I own it," he admitted.

"You own a bar called Savage Hell?" She questioned.

"Um-hm," he hummed into the other end. "It's an MC bar and my club meets here." Dallas didn't understand most of that sentence and she let out a little frustrated growl.

"I don't have time for code talk and games, Savage. Want to tell me all of that in English?" He laughed again into the other end and she was pretty sure he was enjoying whatever game that was playing out between the two of them.

"Sure, Honey," he said. Dallas always liked the way he called her 'Honey' or 'Baby', but that wasn't who she was to him anymore. She made a mental note to set boundaries with him at their meeting, later that night and tried to pay attention to their conversation.

"I own a bar and I also let my motorcycle club meet here," he said.

"And, you want me to bring my daughter to a dive bar where big hairy men who ride motorcycles hang out?" Dallas wasn't a snob by any means but the idea of taking Greer to a bar seemed wrong to her.

"Well, I live in the house behind the bar," he said. "My daughter lives with me, as you now know, and she calls most of the guys in the club her uncles. I can vouch for each and every one of them," he said.

"You know each and every motorcycle riding club member, Savage?" she challenged.

"Yep," he said. "I'm the president of the club and I've known these guys most of my adult life. You and our daughter will be perfectly safe here, Dallas," he said. She weighed her pros and cons quickly.

"Fine," she agreed. "But if anything happens and Greer is put in danger—" she warned.

"She won't be," he promised. "I know it's not worth much to you right now, but I give you my word, Dallas. Just give me a little trust here, Honey," he asked.

"We'll be there at five," she said.

"Thank you, Dallas," he said and ended the call. She looked across the small apartment she shared with her infant daughter, to find her sleeping in her bassinet and smiled.

"Looks like you are going to officially meet your Daddy, Baby Girl," Dallas whispered. "Let's just hope he's worth all the trouble he's giving your mama."

BY THE TIME Dallas got Greer fed and settled into her car seat and drove over to the address Savage texted her, she was almost an hour late. Savage stood on the covered deck, by the front door, wearing his trademark scowl and Dallas thought about turning her car around to head home. When he looked at her like that she was a combination of scared to death and completely turned on.

He walked out to her car and opened the back door to get

her diaper bag and car seat out. "I can do that," she protested and he smiled down at their sleeping daughter.

"I know you can, but I want to help. That's what today is, right? Us discussing ways that I can be a part of her life and help you in the process." Dallas nodded and locked up her car.

"You sure this place is okay for the baby?" she asked looking around the small parking lot. It was packed with mostly motorcycles and she worried about taking Greer into a bar full of bikers.

Savage laughed and looked back over his shoulder at her. "I'm one hundred percent positive you and our daughter are safe here, Honey. I'll just tell the guys you are my Ol'lady and they will leave you alone."

"Ol'lady?" she growled. "Who the fuck are you calling an Ol'lady?" Savage put Greer's car seat down on the porch and pulled her into his arms. Dallas wanted to protest, she really did, but being held by Savage again felt so right, she didn't say a word.

"It's what bikers call their girlfriends and wives. It's a term of endearment and it will mean that no other biker in my bar will try to lay claim to you. If you'd rather be hit on by every man in the place, be my guest." Savage released Dallas and picked up Greer, to go into the bar.

"No," she shouted. "Tell them whatever you want to," she insisted. "Just as long as they leave me alone, I don't care."

"Ol'lady it is, then," he teased, holding the front door open for her. Dallas brushed past him and was hit by the smell of cheap beer and leather when she realized that everyone in the place had basically stopped what they were doing to turn and look at her and Savage.

"Shit," she mumbled under her breath. Savage grabbed her hand, setting Greer's car seat on the closest table.

"Since we seem to already have your attention," he said. "This here is my Ol'lady—Dallas." Everyone started shouting cheers and hello and she smiled and looked around the room as if she wasn't scared half to death. "And." He took her sleeping daughter out of the car seat and snuggled her against his chest. Seeing Savage holding their baby did crazy things to her heart. Things she wasn't sure she was ready for.

"This is our daughter, Greer." A loud cheer and clapping rang through the bar, causing the baby to squirm and wiggle in Savage's arms. She watched as her daughter looked up at her father for the first time and then gently closed her eyes again to fall back to sleep. Greer had no idea what was going on around her, but it sounded as if they had just won the Super Bowl, the way the guys all carried on.

A little girl walked over to Savage, a smile as big as she was on her beautiful face. "This is Chloe," he said.

"Hi, Chloe," Dallas said. She looked so much like Savage, Dallas imagined his sister Cherry and he must have looked a lot alike. Chloe and Greer shared the same hair color too.

"Hi," the little girl said. "Is this my little sister?" she sweetly asked, peeking at the baby when Savage squatted down to give Chloe a better look.

"Yep," he said. "What do you think, Sprite?" Savage asked.

Chloe nodded and smiled up at Dallas, "She's good," she said.

Dallas laughed, "Wait until you hear your little sister cry later—you might change your mind about her." Savage laughed and stood back up with the baby, handing her over to Dallas.

"Can I hold her?" Chloe asked.

"If you sit down, I think it would be fine," Dallas offered, looking to Savage for confirmation.

"You have to be gentle with her—she's still new and very little," Savage said. Hearing the way he was so gentle and sweet with Chloe made Dallas want to audibly sigh but coming off as a lovesick schoolgirl wasn't a part of her plan.

Chloe sat on one of the chairs that she pulled out from the table and held her little arms out for Greer. Dallas gently laid the baby in Chloe's arms and stood by her side, just in case. Savage protectively flanked Chloe's other side, making sure Greer was safe. He looked at Dallas and mouthed the words, "Thank you," and she wasn't sure she'd be able to take much more. Her hormones were still out of whack from having Greer and here she was, standing in the middle of a biker bar, getting teary-eyed.

"Was I this little when you found me, Dad?" Chloe asked. Savage smiled and shook his head.

"No, Sprite," he said. "You were just a little bit bigger—but not much." Chloe nodded and smiled down at Greer.

"Is she your real daughter or is she like me?" Chloe asked. Dallas could see the concern in Savage's eyes and it broke her heart that his daughter felt like she was less because of Greer.

Savage got down on one knee, to be level with Chloe and looked her in the eyes. "You are both my daughters, Sprite. Greer isn't more real to me than you are, Chloe. I love you both the same and that will never change—got it?" The six-year-old looked at Savage and smiled.

"Okay, Daddy," she said. "I'm done holding my sister now. Can I go play with my dolls in your office?" she asked. Savage took Greer from Chloe's arms and nodded.

"Go on then, Sprite. Don't touch any of Daddy's stuff though," he ordered. She ran off, smiling and waving at Dallas on her way back to where she assumed Savage's office was.

"She's adorable," Dallas said.

"She's something all right," Savage agreed. "Some days she's pretty damn cute and others I just want to lock her away and hope that time slows down a little. She's growing up so fast. Holding Greer really brings that home for me," he said. "How about we sit and have that conversation and then you let me get you something to eat?"

"Sounds good," she agreed, sitting in the booth where he had put her diaper bag. "I'll have to feed the baby soon," she said. "Do you have a place I can have a little privacy?"

"Sure," Savage said. "My house is just out back, about a quarter-mile down the road."

"Wow, you live next to your bar?" she asked.

"Sure," he said. "I owned all of this property and when I built the bar, I decided why the hell not. I was spending most of my nights here anyway, so it was kind of nice just being able to stumble a few hundred feet to my front door. Plus, that way I can be readily available for the guys, in case they need me."

"You said you're the president of this club?" she asked.

"Yep, and they are great—for the most part. We're basically made up of military misfits," he said.

"I had no idea," she said. "How could I have spent so many nights with you and not known any of this?" Savage reached across the table with his free hand and took hers, linking their fingers together.

"I didn't give you the chance to know me, Dallas. I'd like to change that now if you'll let me," he said. She wasn't sure what Savage meant by that, but she was too tired and too busy being a single mom to figure it all out.

"What are we doing here, Savage?" she asked, cutting to the chase. "I don't have time for games. Not now that I have Greer."

"I was hoping we could figure this all out as we go," he admitted. Dallas pulled her hand free from his and Savage's scowl was back in place. "I can't go through the disappointment of watching you walk away again, Savage."

"I told you that's not going to happen this time," he growled. Greer stirred in his arms and he looked down at their daughter and sighed. "I was an ass for ghosting you but you have my word, that won't happen again, Dallas. I won't do that to you or to her," he said, nodding to the baby. He reached for her hand again and she allowed him to take it.

"It will take some time," she said. "For me to trust you at your word. I'll allow you into Greer's life—she needs a father and seeing Chloe tonight confirmed to me that you are a good dad. But, I don't need or want to be anyone's booty call, Savage. Things between us need to be platonic."

He smiled at her from across the table and ran his thumb over her hand, eliciting a shiver from her. Damn it—he knew exactly what she liked and he'd use his firsthand knowledge to get what he wanted from her. Dallas was just going to have to remember how it felt to be left. The pain of believing she wasn't enough for any man, let alone Savage. Holding onto her hurt at his betrayal might be her only solace.

"I mean it, Savage," she said. Dallas knew that the only way to make him believe her was to explain what his walking away did to her. She looked down at their joined hands, knowing that if she looked him directly in his blue eyes, she'd never find the strength to get through what she had to say.

"At first, when I didn't hear from you, I worried that something had happened. I called hospitals and asked if they had anyone named Savage admitted and when they'd ask me for your last name, I'd hang up. God, I felt like a complete fool for believing I meant something to you. You used me—I was just a good time, a piece of ass and the hurt and betrayal was what fueled me to get out of bed every morning. Then, I found out I was pregnant and I had daily fantasies that you'd find out and ride in to save me. You know—like we'd ride into the sunset and live happily ever after. But, you never showed."

"I'm so sorry, Baby. I'm here now," he said.

"Yeah," she agreed. "And I'm happy that Greer will have you in her life. But, I don't need to be saved anymore, Savage. I figured it out on my own because I had no choice and you know what? I'm damn proud of me." She chanced a look into his eyes and wished she hadn't. What she said seemed to hurt Savage and that was the last thing she wanted.

"I'm not saying this to hurt you, Savage. I'm telling you all of this so you understand why I can't let you back into my personal life. We can be friends, for our daughter's sake, but that is where this stops."

"Understood," he said, not letting go of her hand when she tried to pull hers free. "But, you have to know that I won't stop trying, Dallas. I'm going to prove to you that I'm sticking around and that you're worth it—because you are."

"You do what you need to do, Savage," she challenged. Dallas wanted to believe all the pretty promises he was making her and Greer but she knew from experience that would only land them both in heartache.

"What the fuck is this?" An angry-looking man stood over their table, looking between her and Savage, his eyes resting on their joined hands. Dallas recognized him from the bar earlier that week, at her friend Ally's bachelorette party. Savage pulled his hand free from hers and Dallas had to admit, it felt like a slight given all the things he had just promised her. He stood and handed Greer to her.

"Give us a minute, Honey," he asked. She waved him off

as if it didn't matter, but it did. She wanted to get up and leave but she was effectively trapped, since Savage and the guy stood in the entryway to the bar, blocking her only route of escape. From the way the younger guy was swinging his arms around, he wasn't too happy with Savage and she wondered what had happened between the two of them. Savage admitted to being on a first date with him, that night in the bar, but this seemed to go deeper. The poor guy was too hurt for only having a first date with Savage and Dallas suddenly felt bad for him. She was him not so long ago and she hated the hurt and sadness in his eyes—it brought back too many bad memories of the past year. Dallas stood and walked to the corner of the bar where they were having their heated exchange.

"I'm not sure what's going on here, but I'll just get going. I don't want to cause any trouble," she said.

"No, you stay," the younger guy said. "I'm the one who's leaving." He turned to leave and Savage pushed him up against the wall.

"No, you're fucking not, Bowie," he said. "You're both staying and we are going to sit down and the two of you are going to let me explain—everything," he demanded. Bowie and Savage were both looking at Dallas as if they were waiting for her to agree and honestly, her curiosity had gotten the best of her. The whole bar seemed just as curious about what the three of them were doing and right on cue, Greer started fussing, waking for her seven o'clock feeding.

"I have to feed her," Dallas almost whispered.

"Shit," Savage cursed. "We can't do this here. Please," Savage begged, letting go of Bowie's shirt. "Just give me a chance to explain," he begged.

"Fine," Bowie agreed.

"Great," Savage said. "Let's get Chloe and head over to my

house, where we can talk in private and Dallas can feed the baby." She nodded and Savage grabbed her things, ushering them both to the back of the bar.

"You two wait here," he ordered. Dallas watched as Savage disappeared to the back of the bar and came back with Chloe. The whole time, she could feel Bowie looking at her but she wasn't sure what to say to the guy.

"Let's go," Savage said. Dallas wasn't sure what she had just agreed to, but from the angry look in Bowie's eyes, she wasn't going to like any of it.

BOWIE

He had waited for two fucking hours for Savage to show up to the restaurant they agreed on for dinner. It had been almost a week since their night together and Bowie was beginning to worry that Savage ghosted him like he had the gorgeous blonde now sitting next to him, nursing a baby.

He finally threw in the towel, paid for his drinks and drove all the way home only to sit around his place getting more pissed by the minute. He remembered Savage telling him about his MC bar and put two and two together since there weren't many bars around town with a line of motorcycles out front in the parking lot. Huntsville was becoming a breeding ground for scientists and their yuppie families, which made Bowie want to laugh since Savage was among the league of science professionals living in the area. But, there was nothing yuppie about his guy. Savage was bad-assed and had the attitude to go with his look. The only time Bowie saw Savage relax and smile around him their one night together, was when they were in bed after he had given Savage a blow-job.

Bowie decided that instead of sitting around his apartment, drinking and brooding, he was going to go out and find Savage and demand some answers. As soon as he found Savage's black pick-up parked behind the bar, he knew he had found the right place. He still had to confront Savage and that wasn't something he was looking forward to until he found Savage holding a baby and the same blonde's hand from earlier in the week. The blonde who had given him the evil eye the whole time they were on their first date. The blonde who Savage ghosted and now, it looked as though he was doing the same thing to Bowie. There was no fucking way he was going to step aside and let Savage ignore him for some pretty blonde.

And now, the three of them were sitting in Savage's family room, while Dallas fed her kid and Savage's daughter played up in her room. "We had a date," Bowie shouted.

Savage winced, "I know you're angry, man but can you keep it down, at least for the kids' sakes. If you need to yell at me, we can go outside and you can have at it," he offered. Bowie wanted to do just that. Hell, he wanted to take a swing at the guy but that wouldn't do him any good. Savage was almost two of him and that was saying a lot since he wasn't a small guy at six-two.

"No," Bowie breathed. "Sorry," he said more to Dallas than Savage.

"I know we had a date tonight and I fucked up and forgot to call you to cancel," Savage said. "But, something has happened and I've had a lot to deal with."

"Don't you mean someone has happened," Bowie spat looking over at Dallas again.

"It's not like that—Bowie, is it?" Dallas asked.

"Yeah, sorry," he said, holding out his hand for her. She used her free hand to shake his.

"Dallas," she said. "And, this is Greer."

"My daughter," Savage said. Bowie wasn't sure if he had heard correctly.

"Wait, I thought you said you only have a six-year-old," Bowie asked.

"I did. Well, I thought I did until I found out that Dallas had my kid a few months back and never told me." Dallas looked as if she wanted to say something but Savage held up his hand. "And, rightly so, since she couldn't find me. Like I told you at the bar the other night, I ghosted her. I was an ass. Hell, she didn't even know my last name was Savage until a few days ago."

"So, how did you find out about the baby between our date and now?" Bowie asked. He already had a feeling that he wasn't going to like Savage's answer.

"I went back to the bar where we had our date and talked to Dallas' friend. She told me about the baby and I put it all together. I remembered where Dallas lived and went to find her. And well, that's how I found out that Greer is mine."

"And, you didn't think to call and tell me. Hell, you didn't bother to even let me know that you were breaking our date. Seems like ghosting is your thing, man," Bowie accused.

Dallas giggled and Savage shot her a look that said he wasn't amused by any of this. "What?" She asked. "He's right, you know. You do seem to have a go-to move when you want out of a relationship. There are three people in this room with you right now and you've dumped two of us by just ignoring our existence."

"I am not dumping Bowie," Savage growled. "I just forgot about our date tonight."

"Then what were you doing, holding hands with Dallas—

you know, if you aren't dumping me?" Bowie asked. Seeing the two of them together when he walked into that bar nearly gutted him.

Savage sighed and slunk down into the closest chair. "I want you both," he admitted. Dallas barked out her laugh, causing Greer to jump and cry.

"Well, that sounds reasonable," she teased. Dallas turned to face Bowie. "Listen, I'm not even in the picture here. When you walked in on us, I was in the process of telling Savage that I'm not interested in a relationship with him—outside of a friendly co-parenting partnership."

Bowie nodded and turned to Savage. "What she's not saying is that you were asking her for more—weren't you?" Savage nodded.

"I told you that sometimes I feel as though I'm living only half a life by being with only a man or a woman when I want both. God, I found two people that I really like and all I can seem to do is fuck it completely up." Dallas finished feeding the baby and fixed her shirt, standing to hand her over to Savage. Bowie watched him with the baby and he felt a pang of jealousy that Savage and Dallas had a connection that the two of them would never have.

"I know you feel the same way, Bowie. You told me that you did our first night together. What if we could try something different—you know, build the kind of life that we want and not one that everyone thinks we should have," Savage was forgetting the lives that they both lived wouldn't allow for them to have the lifestyle they really wanted.

"You're talking about a third, aren't you?" Bowie asked. Savage nodded his head and looked at Dallas. Bowie barked out his laugh. "Yeah, I think she's made it pretty clear that she's not interested, man."

Dallas looked between the two of them wide-eyed and

curious and Bowie wanted to curse because the woman looked anything but resistant to the idea of the three of them falling into bed together.

"I'd appreciate being able to speak for myself," Dallas said and damn if she didn't have the whole hot mom thing down. Bowie saw the appeal of the sexy little blonde and he had to admit, he and Savage seemed to have the same taste in women. If he was going to get through to Savage to drop this crazy idea of the three of them together, he needed to remind him of a few truths.

"You couldn't have a simple conversation in your own bar because your club doesn't know about you, man. How many people know you're bi?" Bowie asked.

Savage shrugged, "A few," he admitted.

"What would happen if you walked into your bar and announced that you are with me?" Bowie questioned.

"I'd probably be voted out as president," he whispered.

"You willing to risk that?" Bowie asked. He knew that Savage was proud to be president of his MC from the way he talked about them on their first date. That was something that he wouldn't willingly give up. Savage didn't answer Bowie's question and he knew he had hit a nerve.

"When you were with me, Savage, was I enough?" Dallas asked. Bowie hated how much hope he saw in her eyes and he hated knowing she was about to have her heart broken by Savage's answer. There was no way he was going to be able to answer her honestly and not hurt her.

"No," he breathed. "I wanted you to be, but you would have never been enough for me," he admitted.

"I see," she said. "Is that why you left me without any word?"

"No," Savage said. "I was being honest with you the other night when I told you that I started feeling things for you and it scared the shit out of me. I wasn't sure how to process everything that was happening between us and I panicked and took off. You were the last woman I was with. I've only dated men since you," he admitted.

"And, you think that matters?" Dallas asked. "You left me without a word and I'm supposed to find consolation in the fact that you only dated dudes since you left me?"

Bowie laughed, "She has you there, man," he said.

"Listen," Dallas said. "I'm exhausted and I just need some time to process all of this." Savage looked down at Greer and seemed a little panicked about Dallas taking her home.

"But, we haven't had the chance to work everything out," Savage protested.

"Yeah, that's my fault," Bowie said. "I'm sorry that I interrupted your—whatever this is. I'll get out of here and you guys can salvage your night." He knew he sounded like an ass, but he didn't give a fuck. He was no closer to figuring out what the hell was going on between Savage and him and now with Dallas in the mix, he was even more confused.

Dallas took Greer from Savage and put her into her car seat. "Please tell Chloe that we said goodbye and we will see her soon. I promised to make sure that you are a part of Greer's life and that also includes Chloe. I just don't think I can give you more than that right now, Savage. I'm sorry." She picked up her diaper bag and the baby's car seat.

"It was good to meet you, Dallas," Bowie said.

"You too, Bowie," she returned. "I hope you find what you're looking for. I hope you both do." Dallas waved over her shoulder and disappeared out Savage's front door.

"Fuck," he swore.

"What did you expect, man? You suggest the three of us fall into bed together and we just agree? That's not the way life works for guys like us, Savage. Sometimes, we have to make shitty decisions and hope that we can find some kind of happiness. You need to wake up and realize that being bi doesn't mean you get to have it all, just because that's what you want," Bowie said. He had spent way too many lonely nights trying to decide what he wanted his life to look like. Sure, he wanted the same thing Savage did, but sharing his life with both a man and a woman was never going to be possible. He still hadn't come out to his own parents. How would he admit he was with a man and a woman to them?

"I'm sorry about our date," Savage said. "I'm sorry about everything."

"Me too, man. I'd say to give me a call when you figure out what it is you want, but I have a feeling that she just walked out of your front door. Don't let her get away again," Bowie said. "If you truly had feelings for her, don't let them scare you off again, Savage." Bowie didn't wait for Savage to answer him. What could he say that he hadn't already said? Bowie wanted him to admit that he had feelings for him too, but that would be asking too much. He didn't want to be told pretty lies and he had a feeling that would be exactly what Savage would be giving him.

"I'll see you around base," Bowie whispered. He turned to leave, not looking back to where he knew Savage was watching him. He couldn't because seeing the hurt in Savage's eyes would only make him want to change his mind and Bowie wouldn't do that to himself. He was worth more than that.

SAVAGE

It had been two weeks and Savage hadn't seen Bowie. He had spent most of his afternoons on base, even on days when he didn't have tests to run, hoping to see some sign of him. He hated that Bowie was avoiding him, or at least that's what he believed was going on between them. He had left a dozen or more messages on Bowie's voicemail and at least double that amount of texts with no return calls or messages.

His only bright spots were the nights he got to pick up Greer from Dallas' place and take her home to hang out with Chloe and him. Dallas had even been gracious enough to let him have her for a few overnights while she either worked an extra shift or caught up on sleep.

Savage had his lawyers draw up joint custody contracts at Dallas' request. She was determined to keep things legal and fair for both of them. Of course, that meant that she would have to accept the money that he kept offering her and he knew she could use it. He hated how hard she had to work to take care of Greer and herself. He was hoping she'd let him into her life a little more, but she hadn't; always keeping him at arm's length every time they passed Greer off.

Chloe was over the moon about having a new little sister and he loved watching the two of them together. Savage had brought Chloe's crib up from the basement and when he put it together in the spare room he planned to use for Greer's nursery, Chloe insisted her sister share a room with her. They had worked out a little routine for the nights Greer was with them and on nights she was with Dallas Chloe complained that she missed her sister. Savage felt the same way about his daughter and her mom, but he'd keep that to himself.

The club had run into some trouble with another local MC. Honestly, Savage found the whole idea of rival gangs to be outdated and even foolish but that was exactly what the Dragons were to his club. Savage Hell couldn't seem to shake the Dragons and they were causing trouble again.

Years ago, they hurt one of his friends, Cillian James. He was friends with Cillian's father and when the family moved back to Ireland, leaving Cillian behind, he promised to keep an eye on the kid. Cillian was far from a kid though, but he was still making some pretty questionable decisions. Savage had denied the kid being patched into Savage Hell and that's when things went bad. Cillian was determined to join an MC and when the Dragons showed him some interest he jumped at the chance to be a part of them, even stealing a car and ending up in jail for grand theft auto. Savage would never forgive himself for letting his friend slip through the cracks —he regretted it still, even almost ten years later.

Lately, a few of the Dragon's guys had been hanging around Savage's bar and when he explained that he didn't want any trouble, that was exactly what he got. Bike tires were being slashed around the parking lot while his club members were inside the bar having a few beers. Two of his guys were jumped and beaten up pretty badly. Savage even received a few threatening notes on the front door of the bar and it was all starting to hit a little too close to home. He worried that whoever was targeting him would show up to his house and go after Chloe or Greer. He called in a few favors with some of the guys and had his buddies, Ryder and Repo, watching Dallas and Greer. He knew that calling the police would prove to be a waste of time. They didn't really take what they like to call "shenanigans" between rival MC's seriously. There was no way he was about to tell Dallas what was going on either. He had just gotten her back in his life and they were working out custody arrangements for Greer. If she knew that she or her daughter were possibly in danger, she'd go into full-on mama bear protection mode and Savage might not see his daughter again. Having the guys keep an eye on them was the best option and one that helped him concentrate on keeping Chloe safe.

His doorbell rang and Savage looked out his front window to find Ryder standing on his porch. He was expecting Dallas and Savage worried he wasn't going to like whatever news Ryder had for him.

"Tell me they are alright, Ryder," he ordered.

Ryder held up his hands, "Dallas and the baby are fine. Her car tires are not," Ryder said. "Someone slashed all four tires and I'm betting it's not a coincidence."

"Shit," Savage growled. "No, it doesn't sound like a random act. Not with everything that has been going on around here lately. I take it she knows about the tires?" Savage hated that he wasn't there to watch her himself, but he couldn't be in two places at once.

"She more than knows," Ryder said, stepping to the side for Savage to see both Dallas and Greer standing behind him.

"Sorry man, but she insisted on coming with me when I checked on her and the baby. I think the cat's out of the bag on this one, Hoss."

"Yeah—" Savage looked Dallas up and down as if confirming for himself that she was alright. "Hey, Honey," he whispered.

"Don't you 'hey honey' me, Savage," she shouted. Dallas handed him the baby and walked past him into his house. He wasn't sure if he should be afraid of the angry woman entering his home or amused by her tough-ass attitude she was giving him.

"I think I can take it from here, Ryder. Tell Repo I owe him," Savage said and turned to follow the curvy blonde who had made her way back to his kitchen. When Chloe realized that Dallas and Greer were there, she squealed and asked if they could watch some cartoons together. Dallas told her that Greer was sleeping in her car seat, but she could sit with Chloe while she watched them. Savage knew Dallas was giving the two of them time to talk and he worried that she was going to do most of the talking. He got the girls settled in the family room and found Dallas pacing his kitchen like a feral animal.

"You want to tell me why you have two of your guys watching my apartment?" She looked beautiful when she was furious, but that was something he'd keep to himself, for fear of having his head chewed off.

"Ryder and Repo were doing me a favor," he said. "I asked them to watch you and Greer and I'm glad I did."

"You really didn't answer my question," she said. "Why?"

Savage wondered just how much he'd have to tell her to appease her curiosity, but not cross the line and piss her off. "You were in danger and I'm guessing that since all four of your tires were slashed today, you still are."

"In danger? Who would want to hurt me, Savage?" She peeked her head into the family room to check on the girls and then turned back to wait him out for an answer.

"It's more who would want to hurt me," he admitted. "The Dragons have been sending me threats and I knew that sooner or later they'd figure out that you and Greer are important to me."

"Well, Greer is," she grumbled. Savage was sick of denying his feelings for her and he wasn't about to deny what he wanted any more.

"Both of you," Savage corrected. "I care for both of you, Dallas. I think we already covered all of this a couple of weeks ago," he said. Savage crossed his kitchen to tower over her and it felt damn good when Dallas leaned into his body as if she craved him just as much as he had been wanting her.

"And I told you why this would be a bad idea," she whispered.

"Remind me again," he demanded. "Because, right now, I can't think of one good fucking reason why we aren't together," he challenged.

"Bowie," she said.

"Fuck," Savage swore. She was right—Bowie was a damn good reason why he and Dallas might not work out. He wouldn't deny that he still had feelings for the guy. Hell, he couldn't get either of them out of his damn head and not having them in his life was driving Savage crazy.

"Have you heard from him?" Dallas asked.

"No," he said. "I've tried to call him every fucking day and he sends my calls directly to voicemail. I'm going out of my mind," he said. Savage ran his hands over his bald head and didn't miss the way Dallas looked his body over.

"I'm sorry," she whispered. "That sucks, but maybe he just needs some time."

"It's been two fucking weeks," he growled.

"Yeah well, sometimes people don't do things on your timetable," she said. "Just be patient with him."

"Sure," he said, "how long will I have to wait for you though, Dallas?"

"We're not talking about me, Savage," she chided.

"We were until you changed the subject. Don't think I didn't notice," he said.

"Actually, we were discussing why your guys were watching my apartment and why some Dragons are after me." Dallas cocked her eyebrow at him as if challenging him to disagree.

"The Dragons are Savage Hell's rival club and they've caused us trouble for years now. It comes in waves and things have been quiet for the last few years. I'm not sure what's changed, but they've been slashing bike tires around the bar and even beat up a couple of my guys. I didn't want to take any chances with you and Greer, so I sent the guys over to your place."

"Why didn't you just tell me to keep an eye out?" Dallas asked.

"Because I didn't want to worry you. Dallas, you already have a lot on your plate and the last thing you need is me adding to your pile."

"Okay, then why didn't you just watch me?" She asked.

"Because I had to keep an eye on Chloe and I couldn't be in two places at once. Sending the guys was my only option," Savage said.

"No, you had another option. You could have let me in on what was going on. Don't you think I have a right to know that my daughter and I were in danger, Savage?" Dallas asked.

"When you put it like that, sure," he said. Savage felt as if he couldn't do anything right lately. Every decision he made regarding Bowie and Dallas had turned into a shit-show. "Listen, I won't pretend to know what the hell I'm doing here," he admitted. "Since going out with Bowie and running into you, I feel like I can't get myself in check. I seem to fuck up everything and I'm not sure how to fix any of this." Dallas snaked her arms around his neck, going up on her tiptoes to gently brush her lips over his, taking him completely by surprise. Savage wrapped his arms around her waist and pulled her closer, deciding it was now or never. He sealed his mouth over hers, deepening their kiss and she moaned into his mouth, giving his tongue access to find hers. He broke their kiss, leaving them both panting for air.

"It's been so long," she whispered, snuggling into his arms.

"How long has it been, Dallas?" he asked. He knew that he was hoping she'd tell him he was the last, but that would be crazy. She was a beautiful woman and he did leave her. She had every right to find someone else but the jealous, selfish bastard in him wanted her to say he was her last.

"Since our last night together," she admitted as if she could read his damn mind.

"Really?" Savage asked, not bothering to hide his smile.

"Really," she confirmed. "Not too many guys want to date a pregnant woman, let alone have sex with her. I guess that after I found out about Greer, I focused on her and tried to save as much money as possible before she got here. I was working two full- time jobs and trying to make sure that I was eating and sleeping enough. There wasn't really time for much else—especially not dating."

"So, no sex?" Savage ran his hands down her back and grabbed her ass, loving the way her ample backside filled his hands.

"Well, not with a man," she teased.

"Wait, what?" he asked. Dallas giggled and wiggled her ass against his palms.

"I have a vibrator, Savage," she admitted. "But, that really doesn't count—it's not like it's the real thing. Still, it was enough to get me to where I was going and well, it was fine —for a while."

"And now?" He asked.

"Now, I think I'm ready for the real thing again."

"Thank fuck, Honey," he growled.

"We still have to figure out what you want to do about Bowie, Savage," Dallas said. She was right—he did need to figure out the whole Bowie situation. But, if he wasn't willing to answer his damn cell, what was Savage supposed to do?

"We also need to figure out who slashed your tires and how to keep you and Greer safe," he said. "You trust me, Honey?" He asked. Savage felt as though he was holding his damn breath waiting for her to answer.

Dallas' shy smile lit up her beautiful face and she nodded. "I do," she admitted. "These past two weeks you've shown me a new side to you that I wasn't sure I'd ever see. You are a wonderful father to both of the girls and I know that in a pinch, I can count on you."

Savage flexed his hands into her ass cheeks and smiled. "You can count on me in more than just a pinch," he teased.

"So, what's the plan, Savage?" Dallas looked at him like he was her fucking superhero and honestly, she made him feel that way.

"I think we need to get you and the girls out of town for a

bit—you know, let things cool down with the Dragons and I think that Bowie might just be able to help with that." Savage remembered Bowie telling him that he was from a little town in Texas and that he still had a house he owned there. It was his grandfather's cabin and he couldn't seem to let it go when the Army stationed him at Redstone.

"What makes you think he'll help us? Dallas questioned.

"Because no matter how much he ignores me, I know he felt the same things I did." Savage thought he was losing his mind. He had only seen Bowie around the base a few times and they had spent just one night together, but Savage had feelings for the guy and he knew Bowie felt the same way. He could see it in his eyes when Bowie stormed into his bar and found him and Dallas together. He'd help them because that was the kind of guy Bowie seemed to be.

"What now?" She asked.

"Now, we find Bowie and enlist his help," Savage said. He knew where to find Bowie. Hell, he knew where the guy lived and he had been a coward not to go to his apartment and confront him. Truthfully, Savage worried that Bowie would push him away and he wasn't sure he'd be able to handle Bowie's denial.

"I need to know if you've given it any more thought," Savage said. "You know, about the possibility of the three of us—together?" It was all he was capable of thinking about since the three of them discussed it a couple of weeks ago. Actually, it was less of a discussion and more of him spitballing, but the image of the three of them together had played through his fantasies each night since.

"Honestly?" Dallas asked.

"Please," he said.

"I can't stop thinking about it," she admitted. "At first, I was a hard no, but now that I've given it some thought, I think I might like it. I'd want to spend some time with Bowie, of course—you know, get to know him. But, if you trust him then he must be a good guy. Do you have a plan?" Dallas asked.

He had a plan, alright. Telling Dallas about it wasn't an option because she would definitely have a problem with the fact that he planned on leaving her and the girls with Bowie while he handled his club's problems with the Dragons. Yeah —if she knew that, he'd be in the doghouse.

"Not really," he lied. "I figure we show up at Bowie's place and ask for his help. He's a standup guy and we'll take the girls with us. No one can say no to those faces," Savage teased.

Dallas giggled, "As far as plans go, that's not half bad. I'll feed the baby and we can head out." For the first time in weeks, Savage felt a hopefulness that he had forgotten was possible and he had to admit—he liked it. Now, all he had to do was just get Bowie to agree to help keep his family safe.

DALLAS

Dallas hated feeling as though she had to constantly look over her shoulder but knowing that someone was out to hurt Savage and everyone involved in his life, she couldn't help it. She must have checked the mirrors for the millionth time and Savage grabbed her hand, pulling it over to his lap.

"You know I've got you, right?" he asked. She did, but that didn't stop her from worrying. According to Savage, they were almost to Bowie's apartment and then things would either go as planned or go horribly sideways. Both girls were in the back seat and had fallen asleep on the drive over to Bowie's. She was beginning to rethink everything she and Savage had talked about in his kitchen. But, being wrapped up in his arms again did strange things to her ability to think straight. She wasn't lying when she told Savage that she had given her and the two guys tangled up together in bed a whole lot of thought. She had dreamed of nothing else night after night, waking up to find her body wet and needy from every dirty thing her mind conjured up. Now, Savage was hopefully going to make those dreams a reality and she had to admit she was curious as to how it might all work out.

She already knew that Savage was a handful in bed. He was demanding and a total control freak. He dominated her body in every way when they were together and she wondered if it was the same way with him and Bowie. Both guys seemed to be pretty damned alpha and she shivered at the thought of them both controlling her every need.

"I know," she said. "I'm just worried that Bowie won't want anything to do with me or helping us. I saw the way he looked at me that night at the bar when he thought you and I were hooking up. He hates me and I can't blame him. I showed up in your life with a baby and basically ended things between the two of you."

"You didn't end shit," Savage disagreed. "Bowie chose to walk away from me and that's on him. I've called and texted, begging him to just talk to me and he's refused."

"What makes you think he'll want to see or talk to us now?" Dallas asked.

"Because Bowie is a decent guy, whether he wants to admit it or not. I'll just remind him of that." Savage seemed so certain he'd be able to get through to Bowie and convince him to help them, but she was less sure.

"Let me go in to talk to him first and you and the girls stay in the car. I don't want him to feel like we're crowding him or trying to push him into helping us," Savage said.

Dallas hated the idea of not being a part of the conversation. She was a part of all this and sitting in the car awaiting her fate felt wrong. Dallas trusted Savage with both her and Greer's lives now and if he wanted them to wait in the car, she would.

"Fine," she agreed. "I'll give you ten minutes and then I'm coming in," she warned.

"Well, it's good that I'm a fast talker," Savage teased. Dallas worried that Savage was keeping something from her. She didn't know him very well, but she had spent enough time with him to know that something was up.

"You sure you're okay, Savage?" she questioned. Savage looked out his window, almost as if he was trying to avoid making eye contact with her and nodded.

"Yeah," he said, smiling back at her. "I'm just a little off-kilter with everything happening and the Dragons coming after my family." Hearing Savage call her and Greer his family did crazy things to her heart. "I'll be back soon—you three stay put."

Dallas watched as Savage made his way up to Bowie's second-floor apartment and in just a few minutes, had an invitation into his place. She smiled, knowing how persuasive Savage was when he wanted to be. Apparently, his charms worked on more than just her.

Savage was gone for about fifteen minutes and Dallas was beginning to worry. She thought about going up to Bowie's apartment and insisting that she be a part of whatever they were discussing. She had been more than generous waiting him out an extra five minutes. After all, she did tell him that if he wasn't back in ten minutes, she was going to go looking for him. Although, Dallas was pretty sure that would do her no good. She checked the rearview mirror to find Chloe watching her from the back seat. "Daddy's not coming with us," Chloe whispered from the back seat. Dallas turned in her seat to find the little girl awake.

"Hey, Chloe," she whispered. "Did you have a bad dream?"

"No," the six-year-old admitted. "I heard Dad talking to Uncle Ryder and he told him that he was going to send us away to keep us safe." Dallas suddenly felt as panicked as the little girl looked.

73

"Tell me what you overheard, Chloe," she said. "It's okay, I'll take care of everything." Chloe seemed torn about what to do.

"I don't want Daddy to be mad at me for spying on him again," Chloe cried.

"Oh Honey, he won't be mad. It can be our little secret. I just need to know what you heard," Dallas said. She hoped Chloe would be able to tell her what was going on. Dallas had a feeling that Savage was up to something, but she wanted to believe all the pretty promises he was making her about them being a family and the three of them trying to find something that looked like a relationship. God, she was a fool to believe that he would want to share her with Bowie and why would either of them want her in the middle? Three was a crowd and she was an idiot for believing otherwise.

"Daddy said that it's not safe for us and he told Uncle Ryder that he was going to send us away," Chloe admitted.

"Okay, Honey," Dallas soothed. "I'm going to figure this all out. I need you to come with me—can you do that? I'll need help with your sister if she wakes up and is scared. Can you be brave and help me?"

"But, Daddy said for us to stay in the car," Chloe challenged. There was no way that Dallas was going to sit in Savage's truck while he ditched her and the girls. She knew he'd go off and do something stupid like try to take on the Dragons and probably end up getting himself killed.

"I know sweetheart, but I think Daddy needs our help," Dallas said. "Can you help watch your little sister so I can help your dad?" She knew that toting a baby and an unwilling six-year-old up two flights of steps was going to be a challenge. It would be so much easier if Chloe agreed to go willingly.

"Okay," Chloe said. "If he won't get mad."

"He won't, Honey," Dallas promised. She got Greer from her car seat and took Chloe's hand to help her out of the truck. "I'm not sure which apartment your dad went into, Chloe," Dallas said. "Did you see where he went?"

"That one," Chloe said pointing up to the second-floor apartment on the corner.

"Good girl," Dallas praised. "Let's go find your dad and I'm sure everything will be fine," she promised. The problem was Dallas worried she wouldn't be able to keep her promise and then what? She trudged up to the second-floor apartment and found Bowie standing in his doorway, door wide open, waiting for her and the kids.

"Hi, Chloe," Bowie said. "How about you go on into my apartment and find the cookies and milk I've left for you? Your snack is in by the television." Chloe looked up to Dallas and she nodded, knowing that Bowie had a reason for sending Chloe into his place and judging from his knowing smirk, she wasn't going to like it.

Chloe disappeared into the apartment and Dallas could tell the exact moment the six-year-old found the cookies from her excited squeal.

"Where is he?" Dallas whispered. Greer squirmed in her arms and began to cry. Bowie stepped aside as if inviting them in.

"He's not here," Bowie said. "But, I'm guessing you've figured that out by now, Honey."

"I'm not your honey," she challenged. "How about you answer my question—where is he?" she repeated.

"He asked me to keep you and the girls safe," Bowie said. "Savage had some loose ends to tie up and then he said he'd meet us."

"Meet us where?" Dallas asked. She started nursing Greer, trying to calm her fussing.

"I'm taking you and the girls to my place in Texas," Bowie said.

"What? I'm not going to Texas," Dallas protested.

"Savage said you might give me a fight, but he also said to get you and the girls to my place by any means necessary."

"What the hell does that mean? I can't just pick up and go with you to another state," Dallas said. She was trying to keep it together for the girls. Chloe was watching her and Bowie, even though she seemed to be watching television. Dallas knew Chloe picked up so much more than she usually let on. It's how she knew Savage was going to bail on them before Dallas caught on.

Bowie sighed, "Listen, Savage knew you wouldn't go for him sending you with me while he takes care of club business. But, he wanted me to remind you to think about the girls and keeping them safe. He said to ask you to help him take care of your family."

"That's not fair," she whispered.

Bowie chuckled, "If you haven't figured it out yet, our guy doesn't play fair."

"What made you change your mind, Bowie?" she asked. The last time she saw Bowie, he stormed out of Savage's house pissed because he had gotten the wrong idea about her and Savage. "You said you didn't want anything to do with me or Savage," she reminded him.

"Yeah well, like I said, our guy can be pretty persuasive and he doesn't play fair," Bowie teased.

"If you expect me to trust you enough to get into your car with the girls and let you take us to Texas, I'd appreciate a straight answer." It really wasn't a matter of her trusting Bowie—she already did. If Savage believed he was a standup guy, then she was in. Still, she wanted to know how Savage convinced him to help them out.

"Let's just say that Savage reminded me that I'm not the kind of guy to stand aside and let people be hurt. I have some time off and I'm actually looking forward to a trip home to Texas," he admitted.

"You have family there?" Dallas asked.

"Yeah," he admitted.

Dallas smiled, "I'm from Texas too," she said.

"Let me guess—Dallas?" he asked.

"Yep," she said. She knew that pushing him for any more answers wasn't going to get her anywhere. His answer was just going to have to be good enough for her because he was right—she would do just about anything she needed to in order to keep Chloe and Greer safe. Even getting into a car with a virtual stranger and traveling to another state. She trusted Savage and if that was what he wanted from her, she'd do it—even if she had a million questions and poor Bowie was going to be on the receiving end of every one of them since Savage took off.

BOWIE

They had been on the road for almost four hours and little Greer was starting to get fussy. He knew that they were going to have to pull over soon so Dallas could feed the baby, but he was hoping to get a little further down the road. Honestly, he had never traveled with kids before, let alone an almost four-month-old baby.

"I need to feed her," Dallas said. "We also need to pick her up some diapers." She shot Bowie a disgusted look and he couldn't help his laugh.

"I said I was sorry about that, Honey. But, we couldn't stop back at your place or Savage's. They are both being watched by the Dragons."

"I'm hungry," Chloe said from the back seat.

"We need to stop and pick up some supplies and food," Dallas demanded.

"Alright," Bowie agreed. "But we can't stop for long. We have just enough time to pick up a few things and then we get right back on the road."

"Will we get to your house by tonight?" she asked.

78

"Yeah," Bowie breathed. "It's not safe to stay anywhere else. I have a decent security system in place, at my house. Savage has ordered some groceries and they will be delivered tomorrow morning. He also said to tell you not to worry about clothes, he's taken care of everything."

"Wow," Dallas said. "He thought of everything."

"Yeah, I guess he did," Bowie said. He wouldn't admit it to Dallas, but he was worried about Savage. Bowie hated that he refused to let him help out with the Dragons. Savage told him if he wanted to help, he could take Dallas and the girls someplace safe. What was he supposed to do—say no? That wasn't an option.

"Do you still have family in Dallas?" he asked, trying to change the subject.

"Subtle," Dallas giggled.

"What?" he questioned.

"You seem to have mastered the whole change of subject thing," she said. "And to answer your question—no. My parents are both gone. They died in a car accident a few years back and I don't have any siblings."

"I'm sorry," Bowie said.

"Well, it's not your fault they died. Unless you were the drunk behind the wheel who hit them and then took off," she said

"Shit—that sucks, Dallas," he said.

"Well, I've got Greer now and she's got Chloe, so we're doing just fine." Bowie wanted to tell her that she had more than that in her life. But, they had just met and telling Dallas that he knew for a fact that Savage was falling for her wasn't his place. It was in his eyes and the way Savage pleaded with him to keep his family safe—Bowie heard all the love Savage had for Dallas and his girls and God help him—even himself. Savage had fallen for them and there was no way Bowie wouldn't help to keep them all safe, so Savage could take care of his club's business.

"Why did he just leave us?" Dallas whispered and Bowie wasn't sure if she was asking him or just talking to herself.

"He didn't leave us," Bowie said. "He's doing what he has to do to keep you and the girls safe." Dallas laughed and he knew it was going to take more than his promises to convince her that Savage was doing what was right for all of them. He told Bowie about what happened with Dallas' tires and his fears about the Dragons coming after his daughters. He saw the fear in Savage's blue eyes and heard the desperation in his voice. There was no way he wouldn't help him. Savage said he was worried that the Dragons wouldn't stop with Dallas and the girls but come after Bowie too. He tried to laugh it off; tell Savage that he was quite capable of handling himself.

"He could have done that and stayed with us. He's going after the Dragons, isn't he?" Dallas asked. He could tell she already knew the answer and lying to her wasn't the way Bowie wanted to start off their relationship. Besides begging him to keep the girls safe, Savage had hinted that he wanted Bowie to keep an open mind about the three of them finding a way to make a relationship work. Honestly, since finding Savage and Dallas together a few weeks back, the three of them tangled up together was just about all Bowie could think about. And now, he had sexy Dallas sitting next to him in his SUV and his only thought was keeping her safe and finding a way to convince her to give him a fighting chance.

"Listen, Savage knows what he's doing and he's asked me to keep you and the girls safe, so that's exactly what I'm planning on doing." Bowie reached across the console and took her hand into his, surprised that she allowed it. "You good with that?" he asked.

Dallas sighed and he knew that she wanted to give him some shit but instead, she nodded her agreement. "Yeah," she said. "I'm good with that and I appreciate you helping us out. But, I have to know, what's in it for you? I mean, you don't seem to like me very much—so why agree to help us?"

Bowie wanted to laugh at the fact that Dallas believed he didn't like her. He more than fucking liked her. "I didn't like the circumstances we met under but I've never disliked you, Honey," he admitted, giving her some small truth. "When I found you and Savage sitting in his bar holding hands, I admit—I was jealous. I couldn't see past the fact that you were in his life and giving him things that I never could." Bowie looked to the back seat of his SUV as if trying to prove his point. "But, then Savage came up with his crazy idea of the three of us and I don't know—it's all I can really think about." Bowie needed to tread carefully here. The last thing he wanted was to clue in Chloe to what was going on. She was so inquisitive and he knew that the six-year-old was taking in everything they were saying, even if she seemed preoccupied with her video game.

"Really?" Dallas questioned. "I just thought you wouldn't be interested."

Bowie chuckled. "Oh, I'm definitely interested, Honey. I just needed to think things through and honestly, I liked giving Savage a little shit. Hearing him a little desperate in all his voice mails was worth it. But, when he showed up on my doorstep today, telling me about the trouble with the Dragons, there was no way I wouldn't help. It's time to stop all the games and find a way forward—that is, if you want to, Dallas."

"I think I'd like that," she admitted. "I'd like to get to know you, Bowie." Dallas smiled over at him and for the first damn time that day he felt as if everything might be okay. He was just as worried about Savage as she was but admitting that wouldn't help their situation. He needed to concentrate on getting the four of them to his house in Texas and then he'd worry about getting an update from Savage.

"What about your work?" Dallas asked. "I'm sure this is an inconvenience."

Inconvenience was an understatement. He had to take the leave he'd been saving up for years now. When he got back from overseas, he had turned down leave, remaining on active duty. It was easier to stay busy and work was a good distraction. Otherwise, he had too much time on his hands to think about all the men and women who hadn't come back. Work was his therapy and not showing up every day felt foreign to him.

"I had a good deal of leave to use, so I took it," he admitted.

"How long have you been in the military?" she asked. Bowie really didn't like to talk about his time in the service or his job, but he and Savage had touched upon it on their first date, so he figured it was par for the course when getting to know someone.

"Since high school," he admitted. "I've been in thirteen years now," Bowie added.

"So, you're about thirty?" Dallas asked.

"I'll be thirty-one soon," he said.

"We're the same age," she admitted.

"Savage give you shit about your age too?" Bowie asked. Dallas laughed and nodded.

"He acts like he's got one leg in the nursing home, but then he turns around and does stuff to make me think he's younger than I am," she said.

"Yeah—he told me he was in the Air Force until—" Bowie wasn't sure how much he was supposed to share with Dallas and how much of Savage's military experience was a secret. He worried he had already said too much.

"Until his helicopter went down—yeah," she whispered. "We talked about it when we were together. I think that was the only real information he shared about himself with me and I have a feeling it was only because I questioned him about the scars on his back." Bowie remembered seeing those same scars the only night he and Savage shared together but he was too chicken to ask about them. He knew firsthand that guys in the military, who saw active combat, had scars and a past they usually didn't like to share—not even with the people they were closest to.

"He never told you anything else about himself?" Bowie asked.

"Nope," she said. "I had no clue who he was or how to even find him when I learned I was pregnant with Greer. I was a fool but I thought that if I asked him too many questions, he'd push me away. I wanted him any way I could have him—even if that meant not asking personal questions." The sadness in Dallas' voice nearly did him in.

"And now? Would you do the same thing or would you have asked more of him?" Bowie asked. Not that it mattered; she couldn't go into the past and change things but he needed to know.

"I would," she admitted. "I've learned a lot about myself since having Greer and becoming a single mom. When I originally hooked up with Savage, I didn't believe I was worth his effort. That's why I didn't push for answers—I didn't believe I was worth them. But now, I know I am. I won't ever be the woman who stands on the sidelines again. Savage knows I won't accept anything but full and complete honesty from him if he wants to be a part of my and Greer's lives."

Bowie squeezed her hand into his, reminding them both they were still connected. "Good girl," he praised. "You are worth his honesty and I promise you that is what you'll get from me too."

"Okay," she said. "Then tell me what he said to you that made you agree to this crazy plan of his," Dallas challenged.

"You really want to know?" he asked.

"I do," she said. "Please."

"Savage asked me to keep the three of you safe. He told me about what happened with the Dragons coming after you. I couldn't say no to him—he was so upset and seemed so lost. He told me that he wanted me to keep an open mind about the three of us—you know, together." Bowie just about whispered that last part, not sure he wanted Dallas knowing why he had agreed to help them. It made him sound like a selfish asshole and maybe he was, but he was done sitting on the sidelines, letting life happen around him. He was done running and hiding from what people thought he should be. He knew that there was a good possibility he would be running into his parents while he was home but that just didn't matter to him anymore.

"Are you?" Dallas asked. "You know, keeping an open mind about the three of us?"

He nodded, "I told you earlier, I am. I told Savage that too and God, the goofball smiled like a lunatic."

"Yeah," she said. "He acted the same way when I told him that I'd think about our situation too. He really wants this, you know? I think it's what he's been looking for but never had the guts to ask for. He's worried about what the club will say about us though."

"He has good reason to be worried. The club could oust him as president and that MC means everything to him,"

Bowie said. "He talks about them like they are his family and I know that coming out to family isn't always easy."

"Does your family know, Bowie?" she whispered.

"No," he admitted. "Like I said, coming out to family isn't easy. I never got the nerve up to tell my mom and dad. Hell, keeping my secret is the main reason for me moving to Huntsville from Texas. It was easier to uproot my entire life than to admit to my parents that I'm bi."

"I'm sorry," Dallas said.

"Not your fault," he said. "But, we'll probably run into them while I'm back home. My house is only about two miles from their own. They are bound to see us and I won't hide anymore. They are just going to have to deal with the fact that I like men and women and if they can't accept who I am, that's on them."

"Well, I for one am pretty happy about who both you and Savage are," she said. "As far as I'm concerned, you are two of the sweetest, most caring men on the planet."

"You don't have to say that, Honey," he said.

"I know, but I mean it. You are going out of your way to help me and the girls and I appreciate it, Bowie," she said.

"Don't thank me yet, Honey. We still have about ten more hours together in this car." Dallas giggled.

"Yeah—now add about six more hours on for potty breaks for Chloe and feeding breaks for Greer," she teased. Bowie moaned and Dallas laughed.

"I have to go pee," Chloe announced at the mention of potty breaks.

"Well, crap," Bowie said.

"Yeah, I have a feeling that my thanks isn't going to even begin to cover it all," she said.

DALLAS

Dallas had spent almost a week in hiding at Bowie's place and not hearing from Savage was starting to weigh on her. She had called and texted him daily but hadn't heard anything back from him and Dallas was starting to fear the worst had happened to him.

Bowie was holding up his end of the bargain, making sure she and the girls were safe, but he seemed to be just as worried about Savage. If they didn't hear from him soon, she was going to insist that they go home because not knowing if he was dead or alive was driving her insane.

"Hey," he whispered. "Are the girls asleep?" Bowie found her sitting at the kitchen table, having a cup of tea. It was supposed to relax her, but so far it wasn't living up to the promises made on the box.

"Yes," she said. "Chloe cried when I told her it was bedtime. She said that Savage usually reads her stories and he told her that he'd see her in just a few sleeps. She asked me how many a few is and I lied and told her ten, just to buy us some time. Where is he, Bowie?" Dallas asked. Her voice

86

broke at the end of her question and she couldn't hold back her sob. She was done trying to pretend she was strong.

"I'm sure he's fine," Bowie lied. "How about we try texting him again?" Dallas childishly shrugged, as if it didn't matter, but it did. She wanted to keep trying Savage until they got word back that he was alright.

"Okay, tough girl. I'll send him a message and I also tried to call Ryder. Savage gave me his number before he took off and if anyone knows where our guy is, it's Ryder. They served in the Air Force together." Dallas didn't know that, but there was so much she still needed to figure out about Savage and Bowie, for that matter. Every day, they were getting closer but she still had so many questions.

"Did you hear anything back yet?" she asked.

"No," Bowie admitted. "It's only been a few hours though. We both could use a distraction. How about you let me make you something to eat and then we can veg out on the sofa and watch an old movie?" Honestly, she was ready to just call it a night and head to bed, but her traitorous stomach chose exactly that moment to growl and she agreed to some food.

Bowie made them grilled cheese sandwiches and she found a football game to watch. "You a Cowboys fan?" she asked. Bowie flashed her a devilish grin, causing her to giggle.

"Yep," he admitted. "You can't grow up in these parts and not be a Cowboys fan. How about you?"

"I don't have a team that I follow, really," she admitted. "But my dad was." She always felt a sense of sadness when she thought about her parents. They had been gone for years now but having Greer made her miss them all over again. She would allow herself to think about what they would have thought about their granddaughter or if her mom would have approved of her choices as a mother. Dallas second-guessed every one of her decisions, wondering what her own mother would have done and not having either of her parents as sounding boards was tough.

"You miss them, don't you?" Bowie asked. He scooted closer to her and wrapped an arm around her shoulder. He had been doing a lot of that lately, stealing little touches and looks. She could feel that he was holding back with her, almost as if he was afraid she'd break or something. Dallas didn't want to push, especially since she was so worried about Savage.

"I do," she admitted. "More now since Greer is here. I sometimes wonder if my mother would approve of the way I mother my own daughter. She was an awesome mom and my dad was pretty great too. I hate that they'll never know their granddaughter."

"I sometimes wonder if I'll ever have that with my parents—you know them sticking around to know their grandkids once I announce I'm bi. Hell, that's if I even have any kids—who knows."

"Do you want kids, Bowie?" Dallas asked. She had started thinking more about what their lives might look like if the three of them did find a way to make some type of relationship work.

"I do," he said. "I never gave it a lot of thought but being around Chloe and Greer has made me realize just how much I do want kids. I just worry that I'll be a crappy dad."

"Well, if Greer's fussing hasn't sworn you off kids completely, I think you'll make a fantastic dad," Dallas offered.

"Thanks. How about you, Dallas?" Bowie asked.

Dallas giggled, "Um, I think that decision has already been made for me, Bowie. But, if you're asking if I want more kids, then yes, I do. Watching Chloe and Greer together is magical. I never had any brothers or sisters and seeing how much the girls love each other makes my heart melt."

"They are pretty cute together," Bowie admitted. Dallas set her plate on the table in front of the sofa and leaned back against him again.

"Thanks for dinner, Bowie," she said.

"Anytime," he said. "I've liked our quiet dinners together this past week, Dallas." She had to admit, she did too. Getting to know Bowie a little each night only made her want to know more about him.

"I have too," she whispered. He was so close; Dallas could feel his warm breath on her cheek. All she had to do was turn to her left and they would be face to face. Dallas made a split-second decision and turned to face him, letting her lips brush over his. Bowie seemed surprised and for just a second, she thought he was going to turn her away. Instead, he pulled her snug against his body, so she was almost laying on top of him, and kissed his way into her mouth. Every little nip and lick made her want more and within minutes, he had her panting with need.

"We can't do this," Bowie whispered against her mouth.

"Why?" she asked. Dallas tried to hide the hurt and disappointment in her voice but judging from the pity she saw in his eyes, he picked up on it.

"Because I don't have any condoms here," he said. Bowie untangled himself from her and stood. "I'm so fucking sorry but I never thought to pick any up and now—"

"Now, you're being a responsible guy and making sure that I'm taken care of," she said. "And, I appreciate it, Bowie." Dallas had gone off the pill when she found out she was pregnant with Greer and she really had no reason to go back on it after she had the baby. She had sworn off men, at least

89

that was what she told herself, so what was the point? Now, with both Savage and Bowie in her life, she was beginning to rethink the whole no birth control issue and knew that sooner or later, she was going to have to make some decisions.

"I'll place an order and have them here as soon as possible," Bowie said. "As long as that's what you want, Dallas. I know we agreed to get to know each other, but I won't push you into something you're not ready for."

Dallas stood and wrapped her arms around Bowie's neck. "How about you get the condoms and then we can talk about the rest of this."

"Deal," he agreed. As if on cue, Greer started crying for her midnight feeding. "I'll change her diaper and I'll meet you in our room," Bowie offered.

"Deal," she said back to him.

BOWIE

It had been another week with no word from Savage and Bowie was beginning to worry the worst had happened. He had put in a call to Ryder and he texted back that things were happening and they would be in touch as soon as possible—whatever the hell that meant. Ryder told him to lay low and keep the girls and Dallas indoors and that was just fine with him. Bowie knew that if he took them out there would be a good chance he'd run into his parents and that was the very last thing he needed.

He hadn't pushed Dallas for sex, but God, he wanted her. Bowie wanted to take things slowly with her and give her time to adjust to the relationship that was developing between the two of them. He wondered if Savage wasn't out of his mind, thinking that the three of them could work. Hell, the chances of he and Savage falling for the same girl was a long shot, but he had. Bowie worried that if Savage didn't resurface and find his way back to them, he and Dallas wouldn't stand a chance. He hoped he was wrong though because the thought of Savage not coming back to them wasn't one he wanted to entertain.

Bowie had called his commander and told him what was going on. He wasn't happy that Bowie was asking for more time off, but he granted it. Taking Dallas and the girls back to Huntsville right now wasn't an option. Not with the Dragons still wreaking havoc for Savage Hell. Bowie had heard from a few buddies on base that things weren't good between the two clubs. He had even heard reports that some of the Dragon's members were arrested on base and he wondered if they were searching for him or just screwing around. Either way, Bowie knew that going home wasn't going to happen until Savage could broker some sort of peace between the two clubs.

Bowie's phone chimed and he pulled it from his jeans, feeling like a giddy fucking schoolgirl seeing Savage's name pop up on the screen. He answered the call, anxious to hear Savage's gravelly voice on the other end.

"Hey," Bowie answered.

"Hey, man," Savage growled into the other end.

"God, Savage," Bowie choked. "We haven't heard from you and we were beginning to believe the worst." Now he sounded like a schoolgirl, but he didn't give a fuck.

"Tell me you are all safe," Savage demanded.

"We are," Bowie said. "Dallas and the girls are all fine. We've just been worried about you, Savage," he admitted.

"I'm fine," Savage said. Bowie could tell he was lying but he wasn't going to call him on his shit. Not now when he couldn't see or touch him. All Bowie wanted was to lay his eyes on him; to see for himself that Savage was alive and well.

"I'll let that lie slide for now. Tell me what's happening back home," Bowie said.

"I've run into some trouble and well, tonight things should be over, once and for all," Savage said. Bowie wasn't sure if he liked how cryptic his guy was being, but he was pretty sure he wouldn't like Savage's latest plan.

"What's the plan, Savage?" Bowie asked.

"The fucking plan is that you keep our woman and the girls safe while I take care of the Dragons. I'll be in touch soon and we can figure out when you guys can come home. Tell me you'll stay put and keep them safe, Bowie," Savage demanded.

Bowie wanted to tell him not to be a fucking hero, but he knew to just save his breath. It's who Savage was—the hero in everyone's story. He was the one who took care of everyone around him and his false sense of invincibility was what would probably end him in trouble or worse. Bowie sighed into the phone knowing that Savage wouldn't listen to any of his warnings. All his guy wanted was his promise that he'd keep their little makeshift family safe.

"I've got them," he said. "Just come back to us, Savage," Bowie whispered.

"Copy that, man," Savage said and ended their call. Bowie shoved his cell back into his pocket and tried to decide the best way to tell Dallas that he had heard from their guy. She had been beside herself with worry and now, he was about to ramp that up by about a million degrees. He wondered just how much Dallas needed to know about Savage's plan. Telling her that Savage was going after the Dragons personally would only make her worry more and she had enough on her plate taking care of the girls.

Bowie searched his house and found both girls sleeping in the room he had set up for them. Chloe insisted on sleeping in the same room with Greer even though the baby was waking up every few hours for her feedings. She said she needed to be near her sister to protect her from the bad guys and Bowie hated that little Chloe understood that they were in danger. He wanted Chloe's only worry to be which baby doll to play with, but instead, she was thinking about keeping her baby sister safe from "bad guys", as she called them.

He walked down to the master bedroom that he and Dallas had been sharing, only to find the bed rumpled but empty. When they got to Texas, she insisted on sleeping in the same room with him and the girls in the room next door. That was just fine with him. He liked having her and the girls close, to keep an eye on them. Sleeping next to Dallas night after night, her sexy, curvy body up against his own—it was sheer torture. Each night, he'd take a shower, getting himself off so he wouldn't give in to his basic instincts to make her his. And, every night, he lay next to her hard as a rock, needing her more and more.

He was going to head back down to the kitchen when he saw the light coming from under the master bathroom door and knew that Dallas had to be in there. He gently knocked and when she didn't answer, he walked in, expecting to find the room empty. Instead, he found Dallas soaking in a tub of bubbles with her earbuds in, listening to music.

"Dallas," he said, loud enough for her to hear over her music. Her eyes popped open and when she realized what was going on, she gave him her sly smile and stood from the tub. Bowie felt frozen to his spot in the middle of the bathroom, not sure if he should turn and walk the hell back out of there or stay and enjoy the show that Dallas was obviously putting on for him. He had almost forgotten why he had searched the house for her and seeing her standing completely bare in the tub, bubbles sliding down her wet body, could even make him forget his damn name.

"Fuck, Baby," Bowie growled.

"I want you, Bowie," Dallas whispered. When he didn't make a move towards her, he could see the self-doubt cloud her beautiful blue eyes and that was the last thing he wanted. Dallas reached for the towel that sat on the ledge of the tub and he grabbed it from her hands.

"No," he said. "Don't cover yourself up," he ordered. "Let me just look at you."

"Um," she stuttered, seeming suddenly unsure of herself. "My—my body isn't like it used to be. You know, before the baby." God, he was fucking this all up; making her second guess how fucking perfect she was.

"You are sexy as fuck, Baby," he growled. Dallas ran her hands over her belly and down her hips.

"I just am—well, more since Greer," she admitted. Bowie watched her hands trace her every sexy curve and outline.

"I don't give a shit about the way you used to look, Honey. You're the sexiest fucking woman I've ever seen. I want you too, Dallas," he admitted. He took her hand to help her from the tub, wrapping her in the towel he just took from her. He turned her in his arms and kissed her wet forehead. He had hoped that the past two weeks had been leading to this between them, but Bowie was never one to count on something that might not happen.

"I've wanted you since that night Savage brought you to my apartment, Baby," he admitted. Not wanting to hold back from her anymore was freeing. He knew he might be pushing her but he just didn't care. Bowie had always denied what he wanted for the good of others. Hell, he had even moved to another state and took a different assignment to avoid telling his parents the truth about himself. In his mind, keeping the fact that he was bi from his mom and dad was best for them so it became his truth and one that hurt him and the people he was coming to care for—Savage and

Dallas. He was done denying what he needed to make other people in his life more comfortable. It was time to take what he wanted and he wanted Dallas.

"What about Savage?" she asked, nuzzling the sensitive skin on his neck. "Won't he be mad about this?"

Bowie chuckled. "Naw, Honey," he said. "This is what Savage wants. Hell, he was hoping that you and I would hit it off and find our way to each other. He's wanted to put you between the two of us since he saw you at the bar that night —you know when you were at the bachelorette party." Dallas nodded and kissed her way up his neck to his mouth. She stopped just short of kissing him as if waiting for his permission. Bowie could feel her breath on his lips and the thought of her being so close again made him instantly hard.

"Did you remember to get condoms?" she teasingly asked, wiggling against his body.

"Yeah," he breathed. "They arrived a few days ago."

Dallas gasped, "You were holding out on me, Bowie."

"No," he said, sounding almost defensive. "I didn't want to push you, Baby," he said.

"Push," she whispered against his lips. "Please push me, Bowie."

"I'm going to kiss you now, Dallas," he warned. "If this isn't okay; if it's not what you want, tell me now." He hated that she held all the power, but she did. He wouldn't make a move without her approval and waiting for her to give it was making him crazy. Seconds felt like hours and when she smiled up at him and nodded, he felt himself exhale, not realizing he was holding his damn breath.

"I'd like that," she whispered against his lips. Bowie pulled her against his body, letting the towel he had just wrapped her in, fall to the floor. He crushed his mouth against hers and kissed his way in to find her tongue. Dallas moaned and wrapped her arms around his neck, pulling him down to take what she wanted from him. He liked that she seemed to know what she needed and wasn't afraid to take it.

Bowie lifted her into his arms and carried her to his bed. He needed to make Dallas his and all he could think about was stripping and sinking into her willing body. He wasn't that person—taking what he wanted from people and to hell with the consequences. Dallas made him want to be greedy and take everything she was offering, push her to her limits and demand even more from her.

Bowie laid her back on his bed and stood over her bare body, looking her over, while stripping out of his clothes. "You are so fucking beautiful," he growled. Dallas smiled up at him, reaching up to pull Bowie on top of her body.

"Right back at you," she said, wrapping her legs around his ass. He could feel her wet, hot core rubbing against his throbbing cock and he just about lost the ability to think straight.

"Condom," he whispered against her lips.

"Hurry," Dallas ordered, releasing Bowie. He stood and found the stash of condoms he had shoved into the top drawer of his side bed table. He opened the wrapper and slid it over his cock, not wasting any time.

He pulled Dallas to the end of the bed and seated himself completely inside of her, in just one thrust. "Fuck," Bowie hissed. "You feel so fucking good." Dallas moaned and wrapped her legs around his ass again, pulling his body down to meet hers.

"It's been so long," she whispered.

"Since you've had sex?" Bowie asked, trying to keep up. He was having trouble concentrating on anything but the sexy blonde wrapped around his body.

"Yes," she hissed.

"When was the last time, Baby?" Bowie wasn't sure he wanted to know but he was pretty sure he already knew the answer.

"Savage," she admitted. Knowing that Savage was the last man she was with made him happy for some reason. Maybe it was the fact that they were planning on sharing her once Savage got done with club business or maybe it was the fact that Savage was his last too, but Bowie was relieved he felt no jealousy.

"Sorry," she whispered, kissing her way up his neck.

"For what?" Bowie breathed.

"Bringing up another man while we're—you know," Dallas giggled, sending waves of pleasure down his body and he knew he wouldn't last much longer.

Bowie smiled down at her, "It's okay, Baby. Savage was my last too."

"I wish he was here with us, now," she whispered.

"Same," Bowie admitted. He pulled out of her body and plunged back in, making her cry out his name. He knew she was close too and he pumped in and out of her pussy, setting a furious pace. Bowie reached down to where they were joined and ran his thumb over her clit. He wanted her with him when he found his release.

"Bowie," she moaned his name. "I'm going to come."

"Me too, Baby," he groaned, kissing his way into her mouth. He could feel her orgasm as it ripped through her core, milking his cock until he found his own release.

"Dallas," he whispered her name and it sounded like a praise as he collapsed on top of her. She wrapped her arms and legs around him and when she gently kissed his shoulder, Dallas stole another little piece of his heart.

"I'm so glad I came looking for you tonight, Honey," he

whispered against her neck. "Finding you in the tub was just an extra bonus."

Dallas giggled, "Why were you looking for me?" she asked. Honestly, Bowie had all but forgotten his phone call with Savage and the reason he searched his house for Dallas.

"Savage called," he admitted.

"And, you're just telling me this now?" Dallas pushed at his body to roll off hers, and he did. Bowie stood from the bed and went into the bathroom to dispose of the condom. The last thing he wanted was a fight with her and judging by the way she was taking the news of Savage's call; Dallas was ready to give him just that. When he got back to his room, he found that she had slipped on his t-shirt and was effectively hiding from him.

"Dallas," he said. "I was going to tell you."

"You should have told me before you distracted me with sex," she said.

"I distracted you with sex?" Bowie questioned. "I believe you were the one doing the distracting, Honey."

"What did he say?" Dallas asked. Here's where things got tricky. Did Bowie want to protect her and tell her only the parts that she wouldn't worry about or would that just land him in more hot water later? "Bowie," she warned. "Just tell me, please. I need to know that he's alright."

"He is," Bowie insisted. He sat back down on the bed and pulled Dallas down onto his lap. "He said that everything should be over in a few days and we'll be able to go home."

"What does that mean—over?" Dallas asked. "Tell me Savage isn't going after the Dragons on his own?" He wouldn't lie to her—not now, after everything that had happened between the two of them.

"I'm not sure what he plans on doing," Bowie said. "When

I asked him, he told me that I needed to promise to take care of you and the girls, no matter what."

"What did you tell him?" Dallas asked.

"That me taking care of the three of you wasn't an issue he needed to worry about. It was a done deal and I meant it, Dallas. I won't let anything happen to you or either of the girls."

"Thank you, Bowie. I just wish this nightmare was over. I need to see him to make sure he's alright."

"I know, Baby," Bowie said. "I feel the same way. How about we get some shut-eye?"

Dallas yawned and stretched in his arms. "Sounds good. Greer will be up soon for her feeding and I'm exhausted." Bowie tugged the covers over them, loving the way Dallas snuggled into his body. She was right about one thing—he'd rest a hell of a lot easier once Savage was back with them— they both would.

SAVAGE

It had been just over two weeks since he sent his family away, but it had to be done. Keeping them all safe was his top priority. The Dragons going after Dallas and Greer was only the first part of their plan. Savage knew they'd stop at nothing to destroy his entire family. The Dragons had done it once and he wouldn't put it past them to do it again.

The truth was this fight between the two clubs had been going on for a damn long time. Since before he was president and he wasn't sure it would ever end. They went after his friend, Cillian James, targeting him because of his family's ties to Savage and his club. Cillian had been paying for his mistake with the Dragons for the past ten years of his life. He was behind bars and Savage knew that the Dragons wouldn't stop until they hurt him again. What they did to Cillian was just the tip of the iceberg. The Dragons were capable of completely destroying Savage's world and he knew it.

Thank God for Ryder, Repo, and Snake. They had stuck

by his side and he wasn't sure what he would have done without them. Savage just wondered if they'd still stick around once he came clean and told them and the rest of his club that he was involved with both Bowie and Dallas. Being bi was something he usually kept to himself. Really, it wasn't anyone else's business, but in the MC world, it wasn't widely accepted. He knew that he'd get some backlash and criticism but that was true in any walk of life. Being different scared people and what he wanted with Dallas and Bowie would be considered pretty damn unusual.

Ryder walked into his office and threw down a piece of paper onto his desk. "They left another note," he said. "This time, Dante wants to meet with you—alone." Savage took the paper from Ryder and read it over. Dante was the president of the Dragons and he was demanding Savage's presence at his bar today, at four o'clock. The word alone was spelled out in capital letters, getting the point across. He wasn't to show up with any back- up and he knew his guys would give him a ton of shit for even considering Dante's proposition. How could he not go when it could end the Dragon's going after his family?

"I'm in," Savage agreed.

"Doesn't fucking matter if you're in or not, man. You aren't going to that meeting alone," Ryder shouted.

"Funny," Savage said, standing from his chair. "Last time I checked, I was acting president of Savage Hell. The club even bears my name," he added.

Ryder shrugged, "Sure," he agreed. "But being president of our club doesn't mean that you get to rule as a monarchy. Last time I checked, we ruled this club as a democracy and I don't remember us taking a vote for you to be able to go off, half-cocked, and do something stupid."

If we put this to a vote, it will get shot down and I can't

waste any more time. I need my family back, Ryder," Savage admitted.

"I know you miss the girls and probably even Dallas," Ryder said, bobbing his eyebrows at him. Savage wasn't sure if the gesture made him want to punch his friend in the face or laugh.

"It's not just Dallas and the girls, Ryder. I think you better sit down for this next part, man," Savage insisted.

Ryder sat in the seat across from his desk and nodded. "Go on then," he said.

"I need for Bowie to come home too," Savage said.

"The guy who's watching Dallas and the kids?" Ryder questioned.

"Yeah," Savage said. "He's a part of my family now too."

"I get that," Ryder said.

"No, I'm not sure you are getting it, man," Savage said. "I'm bisexual and if everything works out, I will be with Dallas and Bowie—both." Savage watched Ryder as if expecting more than just a shrug and nod that his old friend was giving him.

"Say something—anything," Savage ordered.

"I'm not sure what you want from me here, Savage. I've known you a damn long time and I won't act surprised about your news because I'm not," Ryder admitted.

"You knew?" Savage asked. He wasn't sure if what he was feeling was shock or relief. Having someone who knew him —really knew who he was, felt pretty damn good. Savage had spent most of his life hiding that part of himself from everyone around him and now that weight felt as if it had been lifted from his chest.

"Yeah, most of us know, man," Ryder said. "I know you try to keep that part of yourself private, but it's nothing you have to hide from your club. We've got your back and honestly, none of us give a shit who you're falling into bed with, Savage. If both Dallas and Bowie make you happy, then I say go for it."

Savage nodded, not sure he could speak past the lump of emotion in his throat. He planned on doing exactly that, but before he could claim the two people he wanted most in the world, he needed to clean up this mess with the Dragons. Bringing his family home while there was still danger wasn't an option.

"Thanks, Ryder," Savage whispered. "Now, how do we handle this mess? I need to bring my family home."

"I say you agree to meet with Dante, but you do it on neutral ground and with a few of us as back-up. We can ask the club what they think and put it to a vote, but you'll find that most of the guys agree—you won't be going in alone." Savage knew Ryder meant well and he was right—it was how things worked in their club. He also knew that waiting on a vote and setting up new plans would take way too long. Savage didn't have the luxury of time on his side and he knew that sooner or later, Bowie would have to come back to Huntsville for his job. The Army was being generous allowing him to take all his saved up leave at once, but Savage knew from experience that the military's kindness only extended so far. If Bowie had to return home, he'd bring Dallas and the girls and they'd be in the same damn boat they were already in, waiting for the Dragons to make their next move.

"Fine," Savage agreed. "You get the guys here tonight and we can come up with a plan and put it to a vote." He knew he was lying, he just hoped like hell Ryder didn't because this would give him just enough time to get out of the bar and make the meeting with Dante—alone. It was time to put an end to this and get his family back, one way or the other.

. . .

SAVAGE PULLED up to the designated meeting that Dante set up and didn't miss the bikes that lined the back of the bar. He knew that he might be walking into a set-up but what choice did he really have? It was time for him to figure out what to do about his MC's rival.

He parked his bike and cut the engine. Savage wished he would have demanded the meeting be on neutral ground, but Dante insisted they meet at his bar and he needed to keep things quiet, or Ryder would have caught onto his plan to sneak off before the vote.

As soon as he got into the bar Savage spotted Dante. He was sitting in the corner of the bar, a woman on either side of him and when he saw Savage, he quietly dismissed both women. Dante threw back his head and laughed at the way the tall blonde pouted at him, swatting her ass and pulling her onto his lap. The blonde wrapped her arms around Dante's shoulders, running her hands through his long, dark hair and Savage felt like an intruder, watching the two of them together. Dante kissed her and then helped her to stand, slapping her ass one last time before sending her on her way.

Dante waved Savage over. "Sorry about that," he said. "My girls get a little bent out of shape when I cut our time short. They are both a little clingy." Savage wanted to tell Dante his women seemed to be a little more than simply clingy but he decided against it.

"Sit," Dante ordered. Savage looked around the bar to make sure that no surprises were waiting for him. "Don't worry," he insisted. "I'm a man of my word—mostly. I said we would be meeting one-on-one and I meant it."

Savage didn't trust Dante as far as he could throw him

but he'd come this far, he might as well hear him out. Savage had nothing left to lose, so he slid into the booth across from Dante and waited him out.

"Why am I here?" Savage questioned. "I have a bar of my own to get back to."

"Okay—I like to get right to business too, so I'll make this easy for both of us. I know who's been sending you messages and I'm afraid it's a small rogue group of a few of my guys." Savage had already guessed that the Dragons were involved in the threatening notes and slashed tires. Why Dante would simply admit it, seemed strange to him.

"That's convenient," Savage accused.

"Sorry?" Dante asked, playing dumb.

"Well, you just happen to know who's been going after my club members and family and you're just what—giving me a friendly heads-up?" Savage asked. He and Dante had never been friends so him coming to Savage now with information that could help him, didn't add up. In fact, it made him downright suspicious.

Dante shrugged, "Believe what you want, Savage," he offered. "I don't want any more trouble between our clubs and if my guys keep going, that is exactly what we will have —and a fucking lot of it, too." That was one thing they could both agree on—Savage didn't want any trouble either. Not now that his life was finally coming together. Dallas, Bowie and the girls were so important to him and he'd do just about anything to keep them all safe.

"Let's say I believe you, Dante," Savage offered. "What do you want to happen from our little meeting here?" he asked.

"Peace," Dante insisted. "I want peace, for both of our clubs."

"Tell me why I should believe you," Savage growled.

"We've been at this for so long now, why would you suddenly want to broker peace between our two clubs?"

Dante sighed and looked at the two blondes who sat over at the bar, watching them. "You see the tall blonde?" he asked. "She's pregnant with my kid and I guess I'm done with all the bullshit. No more silly feuds between us, man. I want my kid to grow up and not have to worry about being without his father. I grew up without my old man around and I can tell you, it wasn't a picnic. I want better for my kid, you know?" Savage knew exactly what Dante was talking about. He felt the same way about his two girls. He'd do whatever it took to make sure Chloe and Greer grew up with him in their lives.

"I get it," Savage admitted. "I have two girls and thinking about them growing up without me, guts me. How can we make sure our kids get to keep us around?"

"My club's VP took off with about ten guys. They think I've gone soft and they've vowed to start their own club. They want revenge and at first, I didn't try to stand in their way." Dante waved over his bartender and the guy brought them over two beers. "I think if we pull our resources, I can help make this right. I'll own my part of the blame in all this, but neither of us will be able to fight them alone. They're out for blood—both yours and mine."

"Do you have any intel on what they plan to do next?" Savage asked.

"Where is your family?" Dante questioned. Savage didn't make any move to answer the guy's question. Dante chuckled. "I get it, man. You don't have to trust me, but if you've sent them away, you might be interested in knowing that my ex-club members are headed to Texas." Savage gasped, knowing that he was giving away his hand, but he didn't care. If Dante's rogue members were headed to Texas, they knew he sent his family there. He was willing to bet that they knew exactly where to find Bowie, Dallas, and his girls and he needed to head them off before they were able to hurt his family.

"Fuck," Savage spat. "They know where to find them?" Dante nodded.

"I wasn't sure that they were on the right track until you just confirmed it. I have a man on the inside of the dissenters and he's messaged me that they are headed to some small town in rural Texas. He worried that they were going after my mother since she still lives in Texas, but she's in Houston. Sounds like they found your family. You have safeguards in place?" It wasn't really Dante's business, but Savage was done hiding. Not just from his friends and club members, but from the world. He didn't give a shit if Dante judged him for what he was about to tell him.

"My boyfriend is in the military and he's got our woman and my kids covered." Dante didn't even flinch at his mention of having a boyfriend.

"Your club know?" Dante asked.

"Yep," Savage admitted.

"They good with it?" Dante questioned.

"Yep," Savage said.

"Good for you, man," Dante said. "Life's too short to have regrets. Being with two women doesn't even get you noticed in our world anymore. But, two guys? That can get you killed, especially down in these parts. Just watch your back."

"Always," Savage breathed. He stood and nodded across the bar at the three guys who had been watching their whole conversation. "Thanks for the beer and the warning, Dante," Savage said. He held out his hand, "We good?" Dante looked Savage's offered hand over and stood, taking it into his own.

"Yeah, we're good," he promised. "As soon as I hear back

from my mole, I'll be in touch. I'm sending my guys after them tonight. I didn't start this feud; that was my predecessor. Hell, I don't even know why the feud between our two clubs even exists, but it ends here and now—got it?" Savage didn't trust Dante. He knew that playing along with their peace treaty might be the only way he could get the information he needed to track down the rogue Dragons. He would use any help Dante was willing to give him, but he wasn't lying when he said he was going to watch his back. Savage had a feeling the president of the Dragons would stab him in the back as soon as he had the opening. He'd just make sure not to give the guy that chance.

"Agreed," Savage said.

"I'll work with you to stop them, but after that, we stay out of each other's ways, right?" Dante added.

"Sure," Savage shrugged. He didn't know if working with Dante was a good idea or not, but what choice did he have? Right now, the rival president was holding all the cards and if he had first-hand knowledge about Savage's family's safety, he had no choice but to agree to everything Dante wanted.

"I'll be in touch," Dante promised and Savage nodded, turning to leave the bar. The club members watched him leave and he got an eerie feeling that no amount of distance he was about to put between him and Dante's club was going to be enough. It was time to get his guys involved and head to Texas. Savage needed to concentrate on one problem at a time. Keeping his family out of harm's way was his top priority. Once he knew that Bowie, Dallas, and his girls were safe, he'd deal with whatever Dante was planning. Savage didn't buy the whole, "Let's be friends," routine Dante was trying to sell him. He might need Savage now to bring in his club's unruly rebels, but sooner or later the Dragons would be up to their old tricks again—truce or no truce. Savage knew to always watch his six and his little meeting with Dante wouldn't change that.

"WHAT THE FUCK WERE YOU THINKING?" Ryder barked his question at Savage and he stood to tower over his friend. He knew the guy was right, but there was no way he was going to let any of his guys talk to him that way.

"I was fucking thinking that my family is in danger and that I'm the president of this fucking club," Savage growled back. "I won't be told how to handle my club's business and I don't back down from a challenge issued from a rival gang. Make no mistake about it, Ryder—Dante's invitation was just that, a challenge. He wanted to see what I was made of and showing up with you all as back-up would have told him I'm a pussy. I'm not a fucking pussy, Ryder." His friend backed down, even holding up his hands as if in surrender.

"I know you're not a pussy, man," Ryder said, taking it down a notch. "But, you walked into that bar not knowing that Dante wanted to call a truce. What if he had wanted to gut you and send us your body back as a warning. You know what he's capable of, Savage. Don't tell me you honestly believe that fucker wants peace," Ryder said.

"Not for a fucking minute," Savage agreed. "But telling him that wouldn't save my family. I let him believe I was on board and he's going to give me intel on where his rogue members are. We bring down his little lost faction and then we worry about Dante's false promises. That's the way this is going to work," Savage shouted, looking around the room at his guys. "Anyone not okay with that can leave now," he said. Savage paused, letting his words take on their full effect. He meant it too; he wouldn't drag any of his members into his fight. This was personal and he wouldn't demand their help, but that didn't stop him from hoping like hell they'd give it. He looked around at each and every one of their faces and saw the same, determined expressions staring back at him. He had his answer—they were in.

"Thanks, guys," he almost whispered. "You never let me down. I just hope you all will be able to say the same about me when this is all over."

"We're behind you one hundred and fifty percent," Ryder promised, slapping him on the back. "Now it's your turn to let us all in. You can't ask for our help and then take off on us again. If we are all in this, you can't go off and play the lone wolf again." Savage nodded. He knew Ryder was right, but he'd been on his own for so long, Savage wasn't sure he knew how to accept help. He was usually the one giving help, not taking it.

"Fine," he grumbled. Ryder chuckled and he shot him a look.

"I never thought you'd be a dish it out but not able to take it, kind of guy, Savage," Repo teased.

"Yeah, well I am," Savage spat.

"So, what's the plan, Hoss?" Ryder asked.

"The plan is that I need a good number of you to go with me to Texas. I'll be calling Bowie to give him a heads-up, but according to Dante's mole, they will be there in about four hours. We need to make it there in record time," Savage said.

"We flying in?" Ryder questioned. Savage knew that Ryder had connections. They were both in the Air Force and his friend was able to fly just about anything with wings. Flying into the closest little airport would hopefully get them to Bowie's house before the rogue gang of Dragons got there.

"You up for that?" Savage asked.

"Hell yeah," Ryder agreed. "I'll call my buddy at the hanger to get my girl ready." Savage wanted to laugh at just how happy his buddy seemed about taking his plane out.

"How many guys can we take in her?" Savage asked. Ryder had bought the plane when he got out of the Air Force. He started up his own company, catering to businessmen in the Huntsville area and his friend made a good living doing exactly what he loved—flying.

"My girl can hold eighteen with me and my co-pilot. I'm assuming that will be you?" Savage had his pilot's license too, but it had been some time since he went up.

"I'm a little rusty, man," he admitted. "You sure?"

"Yeah," Ryder said. "It's like riding a bike, man—you'll be great." Savage nodded.

"Okay, we can take eighteen guys," he said to his club. "Who's going with Ryder and me and who's riding?" His guys talked amongst themselves and when they had all agreed, sixteen guys stepped forward to fly with Ryder and him. "The rest of you head out. I'll text Snake the address and he'll lead the ones of you who are biking to Texas." As soon as he gave the word, his guys scattered. He wasn't sure if what they were about to do was going to be enough to stop the Dragons, but Savage was going to save his family—or die trying.

"Ready, man?" Ryder asked, grabbing his gear.

"As I'll ever be," Savage whispered under his breath.

DALLAS

Bowie's cell phone rang and startled her from a sound sleep. The baby had a restless night and being woken up in the middle of the night, when Greer was finally letting her sleep more than just a few hours between feedings, just pissed her off.

"Lo," Bowie's groggy voice answered the call. He sat straight up in bed and she immediately knew who was on the other end of the call. "Savage," Bowie breathed. She sat up next to him and tried to listen in. "Hold on—Dallas is right here and I'm going to put you on speaker." Bowie held the phone between them and she leaned in to give him a quick peck on the cheek to thank him.

"Dallas," Savage's growly voice clearly rang through their bedroom and she sobbed, trying to fight back her tears. It had been weeks since she had heard his voice. The one and only time he had called to check-inn, he talked to Bowie. She hadn't realized how much she missed him until she heard him say her name.

"I'm here, Savage," she cried. "Tell us you're okay," she demanded.

"I am," he promised. "I'll be seeing you both soon."

"Don't promise that if you don't mean it," Bowie said.

"Unfortunately, we've had intel that a rogue group of Dragons is the ones causing all the trouble. We think they're headed your way," Savage almost whispered that last part.

Dallas didn't hide her gasp. "Oh God," she whispered.

"It's going to be alright, Baby," Bowie promised. Dallas tried to paste on her best smile for him but he seemed to be able to see right through her façade.

"I take it things are good between the two of you?" Savage asked.

"Yeah," Bowie said. "You good with that?"

"More than good with it," Savage insisted. "It's what we wanted, right?" Dallas knew that Savage had hoped that leaving her and Bowie alone, to get to know each other, might end with the two of them together. She just hoped that they'd be able to transition to the three of them finding their way just as smoothly. But right now, they had bigger problems to worry about. Namely, a rival club that wanted to hurt her and her little family

"We can talk about all of this when you get here," she insisted. "What should we do about the Dragons?"

Savage chuckled into the other end of the phone. "That's my girl, always getting right to the point. Ryder says we'll land in about an hour and twenty minutes. We were just cleared to take off," Savage said.

"You're flying to Texas?" Dallas asked.

"Well, not me," Savage said. "Ryder is the one doing the flying. I'm just the co-pilot. We should beat the Dragons to you by hours, but I don't want to take any chances. Do you have somewhere you can hide Dallas and the girls away,

Bowie?" Savage asked. Dallas shot Bowie a look and she knew what he was thinking.

"Yeah," Bowie breathed. "I haven't seen my parents since we've been here, but maybe it's time."

"Will they help?" Dallas asked. She knew what they were asking Bowie to do. By showing up at his parents' house, they were essentially asking him to come out to his mom and dad. "You don't have to do this," she whispered.

"Yes, I do," Bowie insisted. "If it will keep you and the girls safe, then nothing else matters. Besides, if we're going to give this a shot, then I'm going to have to come out sooner or later. It looks like it's just going to be sooner."

"Thanks, man," Savage said. "I have to end the call. Ryder's about to taxi. We'll be there before you know it but lay low until I get back in touch. Be safe," Savage said.

"You too, man," Bowie said and ended the call. He tossed his cell on the nightstand and threw his legs over the edge of the mattress.

"You okay?" Dallas whispered, "We can find another way," she offered.

"No," he said. "I'm fine and this is the way it needs to be. It's time I stop being a coward. Hell, we've been here for almost three weeks now and I never called them to tell them that we are in town. I've been hiding out here, using the excuse of keeping you and the girls safe, but that was a lie. I'm afraid of facing my own parents and that stops now. Do you want to try to make this thing between us work?" Bowie asked.

Dallas didn't even blink, "Of course I do," she insisted. "I want to build a life with you and Savage." Dallas wrapped her arms around his shoulders, hugging his big body from behind.

"I feel the same way," Bowie whispered. He pulled her

around his body and helped her settle on his lap. "The only way we're going to make this work is to stop hiding. We don't have anything to be ashamed of, so why are we afraid to tell the world what the three of us have come to mean to each other?"

Dallas framed his face with her hands, and she loved the way Bowie leaned into her touch as if craving more from her. "You're right," she whispered. "If you do this, I'll be by your side the whole time." Bowie gently kissed her lips.

"I appreciate that Honey," he said. "How about you get the girls up and I'll call my parents to tell them we'll be over in a few minutes."

"But, it's the middle of the night," Dallas protested.

"Yeah, but the Dragons don't care what time it is, Dallas. They're coming for us and the sooner I get you and the girls someplace safe, the sooner I can find our guy and we can put an end to this mess. I don't know about you, but I'm ready to get back to our lives." Dallas smiled and nodded. He was right and she had to admit, going back to Huntsville was all she could think about. Hiding in Texas had cost her one job and she knew that her employment at her second job was also in jeopardy. It was time to stop running. It was time for the three of them to find a way forward and time for them to reclaim their lives.

"Let's do this then," she said.

Bowie smiled and helped her from his lap. "That's my girl," he said, swatting her ass.

BOWIE

Bowie watched their time, knowing that Savage should be landing in about thirty minutes. Getting the girls up and dressed turned out to be a major undertaking. Chloe wasn't very pleasant when she was woken up in the middle of the night, and he couldn't really blame the kid. He felt pretty much the same way about having to pack the kids up and move them all to his parents' house. Plus, there was the matter of having to deal with their reaction to his news.

By the time he got Greer and Chloe settled in their car seats, the sun was peeking up over the horizon. "I'm hungry," Chloe complained. "Can we have breakfast soon?"

"Yep Squirt, just as soon as we get to my parents' house," Bowie promised. He knew that giving his mom a heads-up that he was bringing Dallas and the girls with him wasn't really fair. The woman had been dying to get her chance at playing grandma. She bugged him for years to settle down and have some grandchildren for her to spoil, but he blamed his military career and told her that he'd consider it—some-

117

day. Bowie knew that someday might never come for him, but he hated taking that hope away from his mom. Instead, he let her hold onto her fairytale dream of him married with a house full of kids. His reality might look a little different than what she was probably picturing, but it was who he was —who he wanted to be. He just hoped his parents would be able to accept that because if they didn't he would have to quickly come up with a plan B to keep Dallas and the girls safe.

Bowie pulled into his parents' driveway and cut the engine, not making a move to get out of the truck. "You alright?" Dallas asked.

"Yep," he insisted. "At least I will be, once we get this over with. One way or the other, we'll be fine, Honey. You have my word." Dallas leaned across the console and gently brushed his lips with her own.

"I know, Bowie," she whispered against his lips. "I trust you and I've got your back." He loved that she wanted to be by his side during this but coming out to his parents was something he needed to do by himself.

"I think you should hang out with the girls and have some breakfast, while I talk to my parents," he insisted. "If this goes south, I don't want the girls around." The last thing Bowie wanted was for Chloe to hear any slights about him being with her father and Dallas. Savage's six-year-old was one sharp cookie and she understood so much more than they gave her credit for.

"If that's what you want, Bowie," Dallas said. "That's what we'll do. I'm hungry, how about you Chloe?" Dallas looked into the backseat and smiled. Chloe quickly agreed and Greer chimed in; fussing, as if on cue, for her breakfast.

"Alright," Bowie said. "Let's get you girls some food." His mother was waiting on the front porch for him, her bathrobe tightly wrapped around her body. His dad stood behind her and they both seemed happy to see him.

"Mom," Bowie said. He held Chloe's hand and wrapped a protective arm around Dallas' waist. "Dad." He nodded. "This is Dallas, Chloe, and Greer," he said, pointing to each of them. "My family." Bowie didn't miss the concern on his dad's face. His mother didn't seem to question anything about him showing up out of the blue with a woman and two kids. She was just happy to have them all there.

"Well, don't just stand there," she insisted. "Come in and have some breakfast." Chloe cheered at the mention of food, causing them all to laugh.

"If you guys don't mind, I'd like to talk to you while the girls and Dallas eat breakfast," he said. Dallas shot him a sympathetic look and he shrugged.

"Are you sure you don't want to eat with your family, son?" his father questioned. "We can catch up after breakfast."

"No, Dad," Bowie said. "This is important and can't wait. We need your help." He didn't miss the flash of concern on his mom's face.

"Of course, son," his mother said. "Let me show Dallas where everything is and then we can talk on the sun porch."

Bowie nodded, "Thanks, Mom. You go with Dallas, Squirt and she'll get you something to eat. My mom makes the best pancakes and judging by the good smells coming from the kitchen, that's what you're having for breakfast."

Chloe smiled and took Dallas' hand. "Come on, Dallas," she said. "I need pancakes." Bowie watched as they followed his mom back to the kitchen.

"Chloe calls her mom Dallas?" his father questioned.

"Dallas isn't Chloe's mom. Dallas is Greer's mom. Chloe and Greer are sisters." Bowie watched as his father nearly went cross-eyed trying to figure it all out. "I'll explain everything once Ma gets back," Bowie offered.

"I'm here." His mother breathlessly hurried into the room and sat down in her favorite chair. It made Bowie smile to think that not much had changed since his move to Huntsville. "I like your Dallas," his mom offered.

"Thanks, Ma," Bowie said. "She is pretty awesome."

"And the girls are just adorable," she gushed. Bowie smiled. They were pretty great kids. He just hated that he was going to have to break his mother's heart and tell her that they weren't his.

"Listen," Bowie started, "let me just get out what I need to say and then you can either ask me questions or kick us out."

"Why would we ever kick you all out?" his mother asked.

"Let's just hear what he has to say," his father offered.

"Thanks, Dad," Bowie said. "I don't really know how to tell you this or where to even begin. I think I've fallen in love," Bowie admitted. Hell, he hadn't really given his feelings for either Savage or Dallas much thought, let alone label them. But, he was pretty sure that if he had to give them a name, he'd call what he was feeling love.

"That's wonderful," his mother cheered.

"Ma, please," he begged. "You don't know everything. I'm in love with Dallas, but I'm also in love with a man," he said. "I'm bisexual." Bowie swallowed past the lump of emotion that had seemed to lodge itself in his throat. "I met Savage weeks ago and we started dating. He's Chloe's dad. He and Dallas dated a little over a year ago and well, he's also Greer's father too. Some bad people are after Savage and they're trying to get to him by hurting his girls and Dallas. I agreed to bring them here, to Texas."

"How long have you been here?" his father asked.

"A few weeks," he admitted. "I was a coward and hell; I

didn't know how to tell you both about our relationship. I've fallen for Dallas and Savage and we want to try to make this thing between us work."

"Between the three of you?" his father asked. Bowie was impressed his dad didn't raise his voice. He half expected there to be more screaming and maybe even some crying by this point of the conversation, but both of his parents seemed uncommonly calm.

"Yes," he said. "Between the three of us."

"Why tell us now?" his father asked.

"Because I'm done hiding. If I want to live this life with Savage and Dallas, I owe it to them both to stop hiding. I want Chloe and Greer to grow up surrounded by people who love them and are unafraid of being who they are. I want to have a family with them and I can't do that without telling you two who I am."

"You said something about needing our help," his mother prompted.

Bowie sighed, "Yeah. The people who want to hurt Savage —they are on their way here, to Texas. They'll be here in a few hours. Savage and some of his friends are flying here from Huntsville and I need a safe place for Dallas and the girls to lie low until we can figure this all out."

"They are welcome to stay here," his dad said.

"Thanks," Bowie whispered. "What about the rest of it?" he asked. Bowie worried that he was pushing his luck, asking for some response to his declaration of being bi, but he wouldn't let his parents just sweep his news under the rug like he never even said it.

"You mean the part where you want to be with a man and a woman?" his dad asked.

"Yes," Bowie whispered.

His mother stood and crossed the room to sit down next

to him on the sofa. "You're our only son, Bowie," she said. "Do you honestly believe we didn't know who you were all this time?"

Bowie looked between his mother and father. "You mean you guys knew this whole time?" he asked.

His father shrugged and smirked, "Yep," he admitted. "As your mom said, you are our only kid. We picked up on all that stuff a long time ago. We were just waiting for you to come to us about it."

"Wow," Bowie breathed.

"So, who wants pancakes?" his mom asked. She stood and held out her hand for him. "I know they're your favorite," she taunted. Bowie wasn't sure what to say. He had spent most of his adult life hiding who he was from his mom and dad and here, they knew this whole time? He felt like a complete fool.

"Don't beat yourself up about this," his father chided. "You told us when you were good and ready and that's the way it was supposed to work out. If you would have come out to us sooner, you might not have gone to Huntsville and you wouldn't have met the two people you were meant to be with. Fate has a way of stepping in sometimes, son. You were right where you were supposed to be when you were supposed to be there and things worked out. Your mom and I are happy for you, isn't that enough?"

"It's everything," Bowie admitted. "I just wish I wouldn't have wasted so much damn time running."

"Well, now you can stop running and bring your family around more. We'd love to be grandparents to Greer and Chloe," his mom said. He almost wanted to laugh at just how hopeful she sounded.

"I'd like that," Bowie said. "Now, let's have those pancakes so I can meet up with Savage. Thanks, guys—for everything."

"Don't thank us quite yet," his father warned. "Wait until

your mom tells you how she's planning a trip to Disney with the kids now. She's just about got it completely booked in the two hours since you called to tell her about Greer and Chloe." Bowie chuckled and shook his head.

"If that's the worst she's got, I think we can handle Grandma here," Bowie teased.

THEY FINISHED breakfast and Bowie loved the way Dallas seemed to fit so perfectly into his crazy little family. He just hoped his mom and dad liked Savage as much as they seemed to love Dallas.

Savage had texted that they landed and that he brought seventeen other guys with them. He really didn't want their motley crew showing up at his parents' house, but his mother insisted. She got dressed and had enough food to feed their small army by the time the guys showed up and he had to admit, it was damn good to see Savage. He was hoping for a more private reunion for Dallas, Savage and him, but that would come later. Right now, he was just happy to see their guy.

Chloe was the first one to the door when the bell rang and her shouts of "Daddy," nearly brought Bowie to tears. She was so happy to see her father and Savage looked just as happy to see her and Greer. He took the baby from Dallas, pulling her in for a quick kiss. When he got around to Bowie, he didn't hesitate, pulling him into his body to give him the same attention he had Dallas. No one seemed to even blink twice at the two of them and Bowie had to admit, it felt damn good to finally be who they were around their family and friends.

"Do you have to go away again, Daddy?" Chloe asked.

"Not if I can help it, Sprite," Savage said, calling her by his special nickname for her. Chloe giggled and sat on his lap next to Greer. Savage pulled Dallas down on one side of him and Bowie on the other, filling his parents' little sofa.

"Why don't I get you boys settled in the kitchen with some food and we give these three a few minutes together?" Bowie's mom asked. She took Greer from Savage and when she mentioned that they could also watch cartoons while they ate, Chloe volunteered to join them. She stood from Savage's lap and turned back as if she worried he'd disappear if she didn't stick around to keep an eye on him.

"I'll be right here, Sprite," he promised. "I'm not going anywhere." Chloe nodded and skipped off, holding Bowie's mom's hand, causing them to chuckle.

"Thanks, Ma," Bowie called after them. When the room was finally empty and the three of them were alone, he was sure he could hear Savage's heart beating, it was so quiet.

"I missed you both, so fucking much," he whispered.

"We missed you too, Savage," Dallas said. She crawled onto his lap, wrapping her arms around his neck. Bowie had worried that seeing her with Savage might spike some jealousy, but he felt none of that. In fact, watching the two of them felt right, like the three of them were always meant to be together.

Savage grabbed Bowie's hand, linking their fingers. The three of them sat like that, soaking in the fact that they were finally together, in the same room, breathing the same air. It just felt right.

"When I found out that the Dragons were on their way here, I worried that I was too late," Savage admitted. "I don't know how I'll ever be able to repay you for keeping them all safe, Bowie," he said.

"You never have to thank me for that, Savage," Bowie admitted. "You are my family now too. At least, I hope that's how you both feel." He suddenly realized that they had a lot to talk about and now wasn't the time or place to hash out the details of what they meant to each other.

"Yes," Savage and Dallas quickly agreed.

"Thank fuck," Bowie breathed. Dallas giggled and leaned across Savage's big body to kiss Bowie.

"You thought this was going to end between us once Savage got here, didn't you?" she questioned. Honestly, he wasn't sure what he thought was going to happen when the three of them were reunited. He sure as hell never imagined their reunion would take place in his parents' family room while a quarter of Savage's MC sat in his mom's kitchen eating pancakes.

"I'm not sure what I expected," Bowie admitted.

"This," Savage growled. He leaned into Bowie's body and kissed his lips; his gesture was so different from Dallas' kiss. Savage was rougher with him and he liked it that way. He wanted every ounce of Savage's alpha side and anything less would just plain piss him off.

"This is what I expected," Savage said. "The three of us are a team now."

"You planned Bowie and me falling into bed together, didn't you?" Dallas questioned. Savage's sly smile told them both his answer. He had planned on them falling for each other while they were away.

"I was hoping you two would hit it off," he admitted. "Sure makes this thing between the three of us a hell of a lot easier if you two like each other," Savage teased.

"I think I might more than like Bowie," Dallas whispered. Bowie took her hand into his free one. In fact, I think I've fallen in love with him," she said. Dallas watched him as if she worried that he didn't feel the same way. There was no way Bowie would take the coward's way out of this and not admit to having those same feelings for her.

"I've fallen in love with you too, Baby," he admitted, pulling her from Savage's lap onto his own. Dallas framed his face with her hands and smiled.

"Thank fuck," she whispered, giving him back his words. Bowie chuckled and kissed his way into her mouth. By the time he broke their kiss, Dallas was panting with need and he wished like hell that they were back at his house instead of sitting on his parents' sofa.

Savage watched them and Bowie could tell that he wasn't sure what to say or do next. He almost felt bad for the big guy.

"Savage," Bowie started.

Savage held up his big hands as if trying to stop Bowie's train of thought. "No," Savage barked. "You don't need to say something you don't mean. I get it—you two have had the past few weeks together and I wasn't here. I just hope you give me a chance to catch up with the two of you."

Bowie shook his head and Savage dropped his hands to his lap. "No," Bowie said. "You don't need to catch up because I already know where we stand. I'm in love with you too, Savage. I didn't ever think something like this would work— you know the three of us? But, it does. You both own a piece of my heart and well, it just feels right." Savage let out his pent- up breath and Bowie almost laughed.

"I've fallen for you both," he admitted. "You two are all I've been able to think about these past few weeks. I knew I was falling for Dallas a year ago. That's why I ran away like a coward and didn't have any contact for so long. I was a fool to think that losing you would make me stop loving you. I'm so sorry, Baby," he said. "I hope you will be able to forgive me in time."

"Already forgiven," she promised. "I've been in love with you this whole time too, Savage. You gave me the most precious gift ever—Greer. I couldn't look at our daughter without feeling like a part of my heart was missing. I'm so thankful you came looking for us. I love you," Dallas said.

"I won't promise that this will always be easy. Hell, I'm as bossy as they come and I'm probably just as difficult to deal with, but I'd like to give us a try. So, we're really doing this?" Savage whispered.

"Looks that way, Bowie said. "You good with all this, Dallas?" She enthusiastically nodded her head, making him and Savage laugh.

"I'd like to give the three of us a chance," she said. "Whatever that might look like."

"It will look like you both moving into my house, as soon as we get back to Huntsville. Greer and Chloe already love each other and I'm sure they'll be happy to be together all the time. Say you'll both move in with me," Savage begged.

"Deal," Bowie said.

"Yes," Dallas breathed.

"Thank you—both," Savage said. "Now, let's join the others and come up with one fucking good plan. We have some Dragons to destroy and then we can go home."

"Now, that sounds like a fucking good plan," Bowie said. He was ready to go back home and begin their new lives. It was time for some happiness—the three of them had earned it.

SAVAGE

Savage and Bowie agreed that Dallas and the girls would stay with Bowie's parents. It was safer for them that way and he'd do whatever he had to do to keep his new little family safe. Dallas protested, but she also knew the score—Greer needed her and Chloe was starting to depend on her too. Chloe didn't remember having a mother, but Savage could tell that his daughter was starting to think of Dallas as a mother figure. It wasn't a stretch. Dallas was a fantastic mom and Chloe loved both her and Greer.

"I want to be kept in the loop," Dallas insisted. Savage liked the way she wasn't shy about asking for what she wanted. She was going to fit perfectly in his little club's family. Bowie seemed more reserved when it came to letting the guys get to know him, but Savage knew it might just take him a little time to figure out that the guys were behind their unusual relationship one hundred percent.

"As much as humanly possible," Ryder agreed. "But, you need to let Savage and us handle the Dragons. We've had problems with them before, but this time it's different."

"Different how?" Bowie asked.

"It seems personal, somehow," Savage admitted. "Their president, Dante, told me that the guys who are trying to get to me are a rogue faction that just took off. He claimed to want to bring them down as much as we do, but—" He was afraid to finish his sentence. The last thing Savage wanted to do was scare Dallas or worry Bowie with his troubles.

"But, you don't believe him?" Bowie finished for him.

"No," Savage breathed. "I don't. Our feud with the Dragons goes back years. I don't believe that Dante wants peace. He might not have sent his guys out after us, but he didn't do anything to stop them either."

"What's the plan?" Dallas asked, cutting right to the chase. Savage smiled at his woman. She was always a get right down to it kind of person. "The plan is we go back to Bowie's place and wait for the Dragon's to get there. According to the last text Dante sent me, they are about an hour out."

"How does he know where his rogue group of guys is?" Bowie asked.

"He claims to have a guy on the inside," Savage said. "But, who that guy is or why he's staying loyal to Dante through all this is the question."

"So, you go back to Bowie's house and then what? Just wait to kill or be killed?" Dallas sobbed. Savage pulled her against his body and Bowie immediately flanked her other side.

"No, Baby," Savage whispered. "We've already called in the local authorities. They are meeting us out at his house. We need to get back before they show up." Savage turned to his guys, "I'll need for most of you to hang back. No sense all of us showing up. It will look like we're trying to cause trouble. I need this to go nice and smooth and then we can all go home."

Bowie's dad cleared his throat, "I won't pretend to know what's going on here, but I think I might be able to offer some assistance," he said. "I am retired from the local police force and I still have some buddies downtown."

"I appreciate that, Mr. Wolfe," Savage said. "But that might bring my trouble to your doorstep." He worried that getting Bowie's parents involved in any of his mess was a bad idea.

"This is already affecting my son and well, I know how he feels about you. It's the least I can do. We're family now," Mr. Wolfe said. Savage felt a little choked up at the mention of them all being family. It had been a damn long time since he had any family outside of the guys in his club.

"Thanks, Dad," Bowie said. "We'll take all the help we can get. I'm with Savage," he added.

"No," Savage growled. "There's no fucking way you're going with us."

"That's not really your call, man," Bowie shouted back. He didn't want Bowie anywhere near this mess. He hated that both he and Dallas had been caught up in the Dragon's coming after him. Savage stared him down, almost willing him to back the fuck down, but he could tell by Bowie's determined smirk that wasn't about to happen. Dallas sighed and got between the two of them.

"A pissing match is the very last thing we need here, guys," she warned. "If I get a vote, I like the idea of Bowie having your back, Savage."

"You don't get a vote," Savage barked. He knew he was treading a fine line but he really didn't give a fuck.

Dallas stroked her hand down his arm as if trying to soothe his foul mood. "I need you both to come back to me," she whispered. "The girls and I won't be alright if that doesn't happen, Savage. I love you both too much." Savage let

130

out his pent- up breath, closing his eyes to take a minute to think things through.

"It's up to you, brother," Ryder interrupted his thoughts and he nodded.

"Fine," He grumbled. "Bowie is with us and I'll bring us both back, Dallas—promise." Savage worried that he was making her a promise he might not be able to keep, but he was going to do everything in his damn power to make it happen.

"I need about four other guys and the rest of you will hang back here, if that's alright with you Mrs. Wolfe, to keep my family safe," Savage said. Bowie's mom quickly smiled and nodded her agreement. She sure seemed to like having them all around, which seemed crazy to Savage. They were a bunch of rough, beat-down bikers. Most of them were either ex-military or ex-convicts and being so effortlessly invited to be a part of the Wolfe family was unexpected.

"We leave in five," Ryder said and Savage suddenly felt more anxious about their little mission. Mr. Wolfe disappeared to make the call to some of his buddies on the force while Bowie's mom finished washing dishes as Chloe dried them. Everything seemed almost too perfect and that was beginning to worry Savage. His life had never been easy and he worried that keeping his promise to Dallas, about them both coming home, might not be so easy to do.

THEY GOT to Bowie's house and Savage worried that his guy was giving him the cold shoulder. Bowie hadn't said two fucking words to him since he demanded to tag along. Maybe he was being an ass, but Savage wanted to keep Bowie as far away from his problems as possible.

The guys scattered around the house, each taking up a

spot to keep watch for any sign of the Dragons. Mr. Wolfe had arranged for the local cops to hang out just down the road, ready to be called in once the Dragons got to Bowie's house. Savage was secretly hoping for a few minutes alone with their new ringleader, Joker, to try to get some answers. Dante's explanation of them just going rogue wasn't quite adding up and he wanted to get to the bottom of this. Bowie had promised his dad that he'd call it in as soon as the Dragon's showed up, but Savage was hoping to persuade him to give him just a little time with Joker.

Bowie followed Savage into the master bedroom and dropped his gear. "What the hell was that, man?" Bowie's tone was too loud to be considered a whisper, but Savage could tell that he was trying to keep his voice down so the other guys wouldn't hear him. Savage turned and Bowie looked his body up and down, and he couldn't help himself. Savage shut the door and pushed Bowie's big body up against it, not caring about the loud "thud" that rang through the room. He didn't give a fuck if his guys could hear what they were doing—Savage had been waiting for weeks to be able to taste Bowie. He didn't even hesitate, sealing his mouth over Bowie's, licking his way into his guy's mouth. He broke their kiss leaving them both breathless. Bowie had that effect on him. He was a complete distraction who was able to turn him inside out with just one look.

"I missed you so fucking much," Savage whispered against his mouth. Bowie sighed and Savage could tell he had reluctantly given up a little of his fight. That's what Bowie seemed to want from him—a fight—but Savage wasn't about to give it to him. Being without Bowie and Dallas these past few weeks told him exactly what he already knew—he needed them in his life and he had fallen completely in love with them both. They were his chance at happiness and his way to find redemption from a past that was sometimes clouded with painful memories and crappy choices. They were his promises of finding forever and he wasn't going to fuck any of that up over some stupid fight.

"I missed you too," Bowie admitted, his pissed-off scowl matching his disgruntled tone.

"Gee," Savage said. "You sound like you mean it too, Babe," he teased.

"You do know that I'm military trained and damn good at my job, right?" Bowie asked.

Savage shrugged as if it wasn't a big deal. "Sure," he agreed. "I'm sure you are very—capable." Now it was Savage's turn to look Bowie's body up and down and he smiled.

Bowie chuckled, "That's not what I fucking mean and you know it, man," Bowie chided. "You dismissed my help back at my parents' place like I'd be completely useless in this fight. How do you think that made me feel?" Bowie asked. He honestly didn't think about Bowie's feelings in the whole matter. When Savage was doling out assignments, the last thing he could bring himself to think about was dragging Bowie into his trouble.

"I'm sorry," Savage offered. "I didn't mean for it to sound that way. Honestly, I was only thinking about my feelings when I told you I didn't want you here with me." Bowie opened his mouth as if he wanted to protest and Savage covered his hand over Bowie's lips. "Just hear me out before you say what you wanted to say next." Bowie rolled his green eyes and Savage waited him out. He finally nodded and Savage dropped his hand from Bowie's mouth.

"Thank you, Babe," Savage said, giving him a quick hard kiss on the lips. "When you agreed to keep Dallas and my girls safe, do you know what I felt?"

Bowie shrugged, "Relieved?" he asked.

"Sure, but not for the reasons you are thinking. I thought that if something happened to me and I didn't get to see either of you again; I knew you'd have each other. You and Dallas would have found a way to take care of each other and my girls. It gave me the courage and peace of mind to do what I needed to do back home. I felt relief knowing that you had Dallas and the girls covered."

"I get that," Bowie said. "But why not accept my help here? I can cover you too, you know Savage. You don't always have to be the badass who goes off and saves everyone else. Sometimes, you can let someone save you." Savage never had that before—someone who wanted to save him. His sister Cherry had tried after his mom died; she was the one who tried to pick up the pieces. But, Savage wouldn't listen to reason and instead of accepting his sister's help, he turned her away and ran as far and as fast as he could. He joined the Air Force and found his purpose for living. At least, he thought he had but then his damn helicopter went down, killing all his buddies. He came home wishing that accident had killed him too, but he wasn't so lucky. Savage wallowed in a mix of self-pity and self-loathing that nearly consumed him.

When the police showed up on his doorstep with little Chloe, telling him that he was now responsible for her day to day existence, he had just about given up. He couldn't do that to her. Chloe deserved so much more than a father who didn't count himself good enough to even draw breath. She deserved the entire fucking world, so he became that for her. Savage turned his life around and learned that it was easier to take care of people than to be taken care of. He preferred things that way and it's who he became.

"I don't let people in very easily," Savage admitted. "I

guess I suck at letting people take care of me. That's always been my role," he said.

"How about you agree to work on that and I'll agree to keep pushing you to let me in. Dallas and I, we just want a chance here, Savage. We want to be a team—that's the only way the three of us are going to work." He knew Bowie was right but that didn't make any of this conversation easier.

"Alright," Savage agreed. "I'll try."

"Thank you," Bowie whispered. He leaned in to kiss Savage and a loud rapping on the bedroom door startled them both.

"Shit," Savage grumbled. "This better be fucking good," he growled through the door.

"They're here," Ryder shouted.

Savage looked at Bowie and he knew his guy was going to give him shit for this next question, but he didn't care. "Give me five minutes with Joker and then call in your father's back-up," he said.

"No fucking way, Savage," Bowie growled.

"I need to know why he's coming after our family. This has to stop here and now. The only way that's going to happen is to get some answers. You can be by my side the whole time," Savage promised.

Bowie watched him like he was trying to decide if he wanted to believe him or not. Savage felt like he was holding his damn breath, waiting for him to answer. "Fine," he finally said and Savage blew his breath out. "You have five minutes," Bowie said, pointing his finger into Savage's chest. "Then I call in the cops."

"Deal," Savage agreed. "Thanks, Babe," he said, kissing Bowie's cheek. He pushed past him to open the door, finding Ryder waiting for them on the other side.

"Ready?" Ryder asked the two of them.

"As we'll ever be," Savage admitted. "Let's go."

BOWIE

Bowie wasn't sure about this whole meeting with whoever this Joker guy was. According to Savage, he was the man in charge of the rogue Dragons and he'd be able to stop the rest of the group from coming after their family. Ryder and Bowie flanked Savage's sides as he made his way down to the end of the driveway to head off the ten or so Dragons who had just showed up. Bowie might not be a part of Savage's MC world, but he had dealt with guys like them his whole life. They were bullies and he didn't much like dealing with pushy assholes.

The guy who Bowie assumed was the leader, got off his bike and walked over to where the three of them waited.

"You Savage?" the guy spat.

"Yep," Savage admitted. "Who's asking?"

"Name's Joker," The guy had the nerve to smile at him, showing off his gold front tooth.

"What can we do for you, Joker?" Ryder asked. Joker rubbed his grimy hand over his chin and looked at Savage like he wanted to do a whole lot more than have a discussion.

Bowie stepped in front of Savage, wanting to send the asshole a clear cut message that if he wanted to get to Savage, Joker would have to go through him.

"I've got this, Bowie," Savage growled. Joker laughed and shook his head.

"I want my girl back," Joker growled.

"Your girl?" Savage asked. "And who might your girl be?" Bowie had a sinking feeling that neither of them was going to like Joker's answer.

"I hear you have my woman—Dallas," Joker said. Yeah, he was right. Bowie wasn't sure if he wanted to punch the guy in his fucking face or let him keep talking.

"No idea who you're talking about, man," Savage lied. "I'm not sure what you are after, but this stops here."

Joker's laugh was mean. "This won't ever stop, Savage. Our feud isn't over. It will never be over. As long as Savage Hell exists, the Dragons will be coming for you." Joker turned to get back onto his bike and Bowie felt a moment of panic. If they left, the local cops would never have a reason to go after the Dragons. His dad put his reputation on the line for them and if they let the Dragon's just ride off, they'd be fucking everything up.

"Savage," Bowie warned.

"Don't worry, man," Savage said. "We've got this." Before Joker could even get his bike started, six cop cars rounded the bend, headed straight for them. "I had Repo call it in," Savage said.

"Thank fuck," Bowie breathed. He watched as cops scrambled to surround the Dragon's members. Within just minutes, they had them all rounded up and in cuffs.

"Tell Dallas I'll be seeing her real soon," Joker said. "You can't keep her from me."

Bowie took a step towards Joker and Savage put his arm

across Bowie's chest, effectively stopping him. "Not worth it, man," Savage growled.

"You expect me to just stand here and let that piece of shit talk about our woman that way? What's the plan here, Savage?" Bowie asked.

"Now, we just need to hope like hell they can hold the Dragons long enough for us to get back to Huntsville. That should send a message to Dante that we won't be messed with," Savage said. "What the fuck does Joker want with Dallas?" Bowie questioned.

"No idea, but we're going to get our woman and figure it all out. Tonight, we fly to Huntsville and tomorrow, you are both moving into my home. I've already put security measures in place." Bowie nodded. Honestly, having them all under the same roof was exactly what they needed. If they stuck together, they'd be better off.

"I'll call my Commander to let him know that I'll be in some time tomorrow or the next day. Couldn't have come at a better time. I was just about out of leave," Bowie admitted.

"It's time to go home and take our lives back," Savage said. "No more running."

"Sounds good," Bowie said.

Savage turned to Ryder. "How about flying us home? Bowie, Dallas, and the girls will fly with us and some of the guys can drive back."

"Got it, man," Ryder said. "I'll call the hanger and have her gassed up and ready to fly within the hour."

THEY LANDED BACK at the Huntsville International Airport a few hours later and by the time they got back to Savage's house, Bowie received a call from his dad. His message said that he heard most of the Dragons made bail and were told to leave Texas. Bowie didn't miss the concern in Savage's eyes when he told him about it. He had to admit he was just as worried, but there wasn't anything that could be done. They were back in Huntsville and for now, they were safe and that was all that mattered.

Savage convinced Bowie to hold off on questioning Dallas about knowing Joker until they got back to his house. It wasn't something he wanted to do in front of his guys or his daughters. If Dallas knew Joker, they needed to figure out their next move and Bowie was afraid that would lead Savage straight back to Dante and his guys at the Dragon's bar. Asking the president of the Dragons for help wasn't something Savage wanted to do, but he did offer to help bring down the rogue faction of Dragons who were giving them trouble. Savage shot him down whenever he tried to bring up the option of them reaching out for help and Bowie was starting to get the feeling that Savage already had a plan but he wasn't sharing.

Savage unloaded the girls' bags from the car and Bowie helped Dallas get the girls bathed and ready for bed. Savage read them bedtime stories and before he even got to the last page, both Greer and Chloe were sound asleep in their beds. It had been a long day for them all, but it was time to find out what Dallas knew about Joker.

She smiled up between him and Savage and Bowie could tell just where her mind had gone. The three of them still hadn't had a chance to connect and he was starting to wonder how this was all going to work between them. Bowie knew that his and Savage's chemistry was off the charts and he and Dallas fit like she was made for him. He worried the three of them sharing each other might be too much for their relationship.

"Um," Dallas whispered. "Are we all sleeping in your

room?" she shyly asked. Savage nodded and sighed.

"Yes, but we need to talk first, Honey," he said. Savage sounded put off by the whole idea of talking and Bowie had to admit, he felt the same way about not getting the both of them naked and trying to figure out what came next. He was hoping it would involve a whole lot of panting, pleading, and a few orgasms.

Dallas pouted and let out her little frustrated moan that had Bowie's dick hard and ready to play. "Can't we talk in the morning. It's been so long," she said, running her hands over Savage's chest and up around his neck. Bowie could tell that it was taking all his willpower for Savage not to give into Dallas' request and toss the idea of talking out the window.

Savage locked his arms around Dallas, effectively caging her against his body. "Sorry, Baby. We need to figure a few things out and then we can play." Bowie felt about ready to pout his lip out too, but Savage was right. They needed to figure out why Joker thought Dallas was his woman and then he was hoping they could get to the part of their evening where the three of them would end up naked and tangled up together. Savage lifted Dallas into his arms and carried her down the hall to the master bedroom, playfully dropping her onto the bed.

"How do you know Joker?" Savage asked, getting right to the topic at hand.

"Sorry?" Dallas smiled up at him. "How do I know who?"

Bowie sighed. "Your fucking this up, man," he grumbled, standing behind Savage. He pushed past Savage's big body to stand next to Dallas. "The guy who came after us from the Dragons—his name is Joker and he says he knows you," Bowie offered. Dallas sat up a little straighter; her smile fading from her beautiful face.

"His name is Wyatt and we went out one time," she said.

"If we're talking about the same guy, he has a tattoo of a playing card here." Dallas pointed to Bowie's forearm. "With a joker on it," she whispered.

"Yeah," Bowie said. "That's him."

"You only went out with him once?" Savage asked. "Did you fuck him?" Bowie could feel Savage's anger radiating from his body.

Dallas gasped and Bowie groaned. "Not cool, man," he growled at Savage. "How about you let me ask the questions and you try to keep your temper in check."

"What?" Savage defended. "It's an honest question."

"Then I'll give you an honest answer," Dallas spat, standing from the bed to face Savage square on. Bowie loved that their woman could give as good as she got. She'd never back down from Savage's growly nature and that was something they both needed in their lives. She'd always call them both on their shit. "I dated him after you ghosted me and like I've already told you, you were the last man I had sex with— well, until Bowie."

Bowie smiled down at her and pulled her against his body, hoping to deflect some of the tension in the air. "Thanks, Baby," he whispered and kissed her forehead. Dallas leaned into his body and looked over at Savage as if challenging him to dispute what she said. Savage broke out into a fit of laughter and Dallas looked between him and Bowie as if she couldn't figure out if he'd lost his mind. Bowie was thinking the same thing, worried that all the stress had finally caught up to their guy.

"Savage," Dallas soothed. She sounded like she was trying to talk down a feral animal. "You okay?" Savage gasped for air and every time he tried to get himself under control, his laughing fits started all over again.

Bowie sat down on the bed, pulling Dallas onto his lap.

"Let's just give him some time, Honey," Bowie offered. They watched as Savage tried, really tried to get himself together. At the end of a few minutes of uncontrolled laughter, he stood in front of them both, tears streaming down his cheeks, panting for air.

"Now then," Bowie started. "Care to share what's so funny?" He cocked an eyebrow at Savage and frowned when his guy cracked a smile. "Oh no," he barked. "Don't start that again. Spill it," Bowie ordered.

"You two," Savage said. "You both couldn't even stand being in the same room when you first met and now, here we are, Dallas turning to you for protection and comfort. It's just funny, I guess. At least, I thought it was."

"Isn't this what you wanted, Savage?" Dallas questioned. "You told Bowie you wanted to put me between you, right?" Savage sobered at her mention of her being between the two of them, pulling her from Bowie's lap and into his arms.

"Yes," He admitted. "I want this more than anything—the three of us. But, I also need to know what happened between you and Joker, if I'm going to keep everyone safe."

"We, Savage. You keep forgetting that you aren't alone in all this. We're going to keep everyone safe," Bowie challenged, standing to frame Dallas' body with his own. Savage was right about one thing; their woman did fit pretty damn well between the two of them.

"I swear, it was just one date. Heck, it wasn't even a real date. He took me to a dive bar with the worst burgers and I ended up paying my half of the bill. At the end of night, I made up some excuse about having to meet an old friend and when he tried to kiss me, I shot him down. My only saving grace was that we were in public and he didn't dare force himself on me. If we were alone," Dallas said, shuttering at the thought. They both wrapped an arm around her, giving her comfort. "You have to believe me, Savage. It wasn't anything more."

"I believe you, Baby," he admitted. "Did you tell Joker that you were pregnant?"

"No," she said. "I didn't know yet. I agreed to go out with him two weeks after you ghosted me. Honestly, I had no desire to go out with him but he kept showing up at my work—the waitressing gig I used to have, and he just wouldn't take no for an answer. After our date, he kept coming around and when I wasn't working, he tried to get the other waitresses to give him my phone number. When they refused, he figured out my schedule and started coming in when I was working. One night, he tried to follow me home, but I caught on and led him on a wild goose chase." Dallas giggled. "We got to the Tennessee border and I guess he caught on to me and he turned around. I had to quit my job and find another one, which was no easy feat. I had figured out I was pregnant by that point and the morning sickness was more like morning, noon and night sickness. Working two jobs became a challenge and convincing my new boss to keep giving me second chances when I didn't show up for my shift was a tough sell."

"I'm so sorry, Baby," Savage said. Bowie knew that Savage was still beating himself up for ghosting Dallas and not knowing about Greer until she was almost three months old. It was something the two of them were going to have to continue to work through, but Dallas was so forgiving. Bowie knew that Savage would treat her like a fucking princess from now on. Honestly, he felt the same way about her. If Dallas allowed, they'd make sure she never had to work again, but that would mean her letting them take care of her and the girls. It was going to be a fight given how independent Dallas was.

"I already told you that I forgive you for all of that, Savage. We're all here now and that's all that matters—the future and finding our way forward, together," Dallas said.

"She's right, man," Bowie whispered. "We need to forget all the shit in our pasts and figure out our future, together."

"Thank you—both," Savage said.

"What are we going to do about Joker?" Dallas asked.

"I think I need to go in and have another meeting with Dante," Savage said. Bowie groaned, knowing that he might say that. "It's the only way, Bowie. If he wants Joker and his motley crew out of the picture, as badly as he claims to, then he'll help me to bring them down."

"Promise me you'll give it a day or two before you set up the meeting. Let's not be too hasty in running to Dante for help," Bowie said. "You said yourself you don't trust the guy."

"I don't," Savage admitted.

"Then don't call him yet," Bowie begged. He knew he was asking for a lot. Savage was a take-charge kind of guy and storming into the Dragon's bar to demand answers was just his style. It was also a good way to get himself killed. Bowie just needed a little time to come up with other options and stalling Savage was his only hope.

Savage nodded, "Fine," he agreed. "But, just a day or two and then I'm setting up the meeting."

"Thanks, man," Bowie said. "Now can we get to the part of the evening where we get naked and make our girl shout out our names?" Dallas seemed to perk up at the mention of them all getting naked, even going the extra mile to squeal and bounce around on Bowie's lap.

"I'd say our woman approves of your plan, Babe," Savage teased.

"Yes," Dallas agreed. "She does."

DALLAS

Dallas watched the exchange of power between her two guys and she had to admit, it was fascinating. Savage was so dominant but being with Bowie, one on one showed her just how dominant he was too. She had fantasized about both of them together and wondered which one of them would end up as the alpha. Her biggest question was who was going to be her dominant and if she'd always play the submissive. Honestly, that was just fine with her. She liked it when both guys got growly and bossy with her. Dallas wasn't sure she'd be able to handle both of their dominance, but it would be a lot of fun trying to figure it out.

She watched as Savage pushed Bowie up against the wall and kissed his way into his mouth. It was the hottest thing she had ever seen. Savage was harder with Bowie than he was with her. He broke their kiss, leaving them both panting for air.

"Come here, Dallas," he ordered. She didn't hesitate, getting up from the bed and crossing the room to where they were both pressed up against each other. "You like watching us, don't you?" Savage asked.

"Yes," she breathed. "It's hot as hell."

"Kiss Bowie," Savage ordered. Dallas smiled and wrapped her arms around Bowie's neck, going up on her tiptoes to gently brush her lips against his.

"Fuck," Savage growled. Dallas stopped kissing Bowie and took a step back from him, worried she had done something wrong.

"What did I do wrong?" she asked.

"You didn't do anything wrong, Honey," Bowie offered. "In fact, I'm betting you did everything right. I think our guy just realized how hot it is to watch us together. Were you worried you would feel jealous?" Bowie asked Savage.

Savage shyly nodded. "I did," he admitted. "But, I don't—at all," he quickly added. "Watching the two of you together just feels natural; it feels right."

"It does, doesn't it?" Dallas asked. She turned and faced Savage, wrapping her arms around his shoulders to give him the same attention. His kiss was so different from Bowie's. He wasn't as rough with her as he was with Bowie, but Savage kissed her mouth like a starving man. Dallas moaned into his mouth and Savage walked her backward, pushing her body up against the wall to stand next to Bowie. Savage's body was so big he was able to block both her and Bowie against the wall, framing his hands on either side of them. After he got done kissing Dallas, he worked his way over to Bowie. She couldn't take anymore, she needed to touch them both.

"Please, Savage," she begged. "Can I touch you?" It had been so long since she was with him and not feeling him, touching him, taking what she needed from Savage felt like a denial.

"Yes, Baby," he agreed. "You can touch both of us." Dallas flashed them both her wicked grin and unbuttoned Savage's waistband, dipping both of her hands down into his pants to find his heavy shaft.

"No underwear still?" she chided. She wanted to sound as if she was scolding him, but Dallas found it hot that Savage never wore underwear.

"He doesn't own any," Bowie breathed. Dallas could tell that he was on edge, waiting to see if she'd give him the same attention she was giving to Savage.

"Bowie," she whispered against his lips. She pulled her hands from Savage's cock, causing him to groan out his displeasure, and dipped her hands into Bowie's sweatpants, finding his cock hard and ready. He moaned into her mouth and Dallas was ready for more. She sunk to her knees and leaned back on her calves, waiting for Savage to give her what she wanted.

"Open," he ordered. Savage pulled his cock free and slid it into her willing mouth, to the back of her throat. She loved the way he took complete control of her offered mouth, sliding in and out, letting her tongue play with the tip.

"Fuck," Bowie swore. She looked over to find him palming his own cock, watching her suck Savage in and out. He pulled free from her mouth and Dallas protested.

"Bowie's turn, Honey," Savage hoarsely ordered. She nodded and opened her mouth for Bowie. He slid to the back of her throat and she swallowed around his cock, just the way she knew he liked it.

"I'm going to fucking come down her pretty throat," Bowie said. Savage nodded down at her and she knew he was giving her the go-ahead to make that happen. Savage kissed Bowie and she could feel that he was close. Dallas reached her hand up to grab Savage's shaft, stroking him as she felt Bowie's release slide down her throat.

"Fuck," Bowie swore. "That was so fucking good, Baby," he praised.

"My turn," Savage ordered. His throbbing cock felt as if it was about ready to burst in her hands. Savage turned to face her again, pushing back into her mouth. He groaned and stilled. "Shit," he growled. Dallas could hardly breathe around his massive cock and when he pulled out, she quickly took a breath, knowing that he was going to push all the way back into her mouth again. That continued for a few more thrusts and just when she was sure she wasn't going to be able to take any more, he came in hot spurts down her throat.

"Baby," Savage soothed, running his hand down her jaw to gently cup her chin. He ran the pad of his thumb over her bottom lip, wiping up his seed and Dallas pulled it back into her mouth to lick it off his finger. She wanted all of him and judging from the sexy smirk on his face, he was pleased.

"Good girl," Savage praised. "Strip her," he said to Bowie. Dallas watched as both her guys finished getting naked and then Bowie shot her a wolfish grin. He was about to do what Savage had ordered and so much more if the look on his face was any indication.

"Up on the bed, Honey," Bowie ordered.

"Do I take orders from both of you then?" she stuttered.

"Yes," Savage said, giving her ass a swat. "Now, do as our guy tells you and get that sweet ass on our bed." She stood from the floor and climbed up onto the bed. Bowie pulled her leggings down her body, taking her panties with them. Savage sat in the corner chair watching Bowie get her naked and she liked the way he couldn't seem to take his eyes off her. His stare felt like a personal touch as his eyes roamed her body, inch by inch.

"Savage," she whispered.

"Shh, Honey," he said. "Let Bowie take care of you while I watch." Bowie pulled her t-shirt over her head and hissed out his breath.

"No bra," he said, making a tsking noise. "You are a complete tease."

"Am not," she said. "It's easier to feed Greer this way." Dallas palmed her own breasts and Bowie pulled her hands free and pinned them above her head.

"Touching you is our job," he said. Bowie kissed his way down her body and Dallas was having a hard time holding still. His hands and his lips felt so good, she couldn't take much more. Dallas needed to get off and she'd do just about anything for an orgasm, including begging. Her voice sounded needy and breathless, even to her own ears. She looked over to the corner of the room where Savage sat completely naked in the big armchair, leaning back, watching them.

"Eat her pussy," Savage growled. "Get our girl off, Bowie and then, I'm going to fuck your ass while you fuck her." She and Bowie moaned in unison. He seemed to like Savage's idea as much as she had. Dallas looked down her body to where Bowie had settled between her legs and laid back against the mattress as if it was all too much to watch.

"You smell so fucking good, Baby," Bowie whispered. She could feel his hot breath on her wet folds and she knew what he was going to do next. He parted her legs and licked her pussy, sucking her sensitive nub into his mouth. Dallas bucked and thrashed against Bowie's mouth.

"I'll hold her still," Savage offered. He stood from his corner perch and Dallas watched him saunter across the room. He practically crawled on top of her body, trapping her under him. Savage held her down while Bowie lapped and sucked at her drenched folds until she closed her eyes and was sure she could literally see stars. Just when she was about to come, Savage sealed his mouth over her own, stealing her shouts and moans.

Bowie stood and wiped his mouth on his forearm, smiling down at the two of them. "So fucking good," he taunted. Savage stood and went to the nightstand to find the lube. Bowie didn't give her any time to recover from her mind-numbing orgasm, he pulled her to the edge of the bed and sunk into her body, sliding easily through her wet folds.

"Yes," he hissed. Savage stood behind Bowie, a triumphant smile on his handsome face as he held up the lube. Dallas giggled and Bowie seemed to like the sensation until Savage pushed his body down onto her own and started rubbing lube into his ass. She watched fascinated by the exchange of power between Savage and Bowie.

"You're going to feel so good, Babe," Savage said to Bowie. He moaned and sucked one of Dallas' nipples into his hot mouth.

"Do you like what he's doing to you, Bowie?" Dallas questioned.

"Yes," Bowie moaned. "I need more, Savage." As if on cue, Savage tossed the lube onto the bed and stood behind him. Dallas could tell the exact moment that Savage shoved into Bowie's ass. She suddenly felt fuller and Bowie stilled inside of her as if he needed a minute to adjust to the new sensations.

"Fuck," Savage moaned.

"Fucking right," Bowie growled. "Move, please," he begged. Savage set a punishing pace and it didn't take Dallas long to find her release again. Bowie quickly followed her over and a few thrusts later, Savage pumped his own release into Bowie's ass. They collapsed together onto the king-size bed and Dallas wasn't sure she had ever felt so completely loved in her whole life.

She expected to feel differently, being with two men at once, but that wasn't the case. Bowie and Savage weren't who she expected. Being with the two of them felt right—like coming home and for just a minute, Dallas let herself believe that the three of them would be able to find their way together. Savage and Bowie were hers and she was now theirs—body, mind and soul and Dallas wouldn't want it any other way.

SAVAGE

Dallas, Bowie and he had spent every waking hour together for the past two days. When the girls were awake, they tried to make everything as normal as possible for them. He wanted Chloe to get to know the three of them as a family unit. He wanted her to trust Dallas and Bowie as much as he had come to. But, most of all, he wanted her to love them as much as he did. Savage wanted the five of them to be a family, but he also knew not to push his daughter into accepting something she might not want to. Chloe was still so young; he didn't expect her to understand the ins and outs of their relationship. All Savage could really hope for was both of his daughters to feel safe and completely loved—the rest would come.

Every night when the girls went to bed, the three of them locked themselves away in their room and found new ways to make each other crazy. Their relationship was exciting and new and Savage wasn't sure how he had gotten so lucky in finding the two people on the planet who seemed to complete him.

Bowie came running into the bar and motioned for Savage to meet him in his office. He excused himself from behind the bar and threw his new bartender, Whisky, his towel. "You got this, man?" Savage asked Whisky.

"No sweat, man," Whisky said, his smile easy. Savage liked the new guy and he had to admit, he knew his stuff. Most guys that came into Savage Hell ordered a beer or shots, but Whisky knew how to make a mean martini and he was quickly becoming popular with the biker's ol'ladies who liked to ask for fancy mixed drinks. Whiskey was ex-military and a few years younger than Savage. He just got back from a long stint in Mexico and Savage wondered what the guy's story was. He seemed friendly enough but there was something behind Whisky's eyes that told another story.

"Thanks, man," Savage said. "I won't be too long." He walked back the narrow hallway to his office and found Bowie pacing the floor in front of his desk.

"What's up, Babe?" Savage asked, shutting the door on his way into the office. "You look about ready to crawl out of your skin. Dallas and the girls okay?" Savage had left them all home this afternoon, after Bowie got off work early, surprising them all with Asian takeout.

"Yeah, they are fine. Dallas is feeding Greer and Chloe is taking her bath, getting ready for bed. It's something else," Bowie said. Savage nodded for him to go on, hating the suspense. "My dad called. He went over to check my house, you know just to make sure everything was secure, and he found a body on my back patio."

"What the fuck?" Savage shouted. "Who's body?"

"He called in a few favors and I'm not supposed to know this, but it looks like the guy was a Dragon. His name was Chris Sharp but he had the name Stinger on his cut."

"Shit," Savage growled. "I know Stinger. He wasn't a bad guy. In fact, he tried to patch into Savage Hell but changed his mind at the last minute and joined the Dragons. It was about the same time as my friend, Cillian James tried to patch in with them. He got caught stealing a car and is still in prison. Stinger and Cillian were friends," Savage said. He knew he was going to have to make a trip up to the county jail to tell his friend about Stinger, but they had bigger problems right now. Namely, why a dead Dragon would end up in Bowie's backyard.

"Your dad have any idea why his body was dumped at your house?" Savage questioned.

"No," Bowie said. "He had the word "Traitor" carved into his chest. Could he be Dante's lookout?"

"Sounds about right," Savage agreed. "What did the cops say?"

"For now, they'll let my dad handle things for me since they know him. I need to go in, to give my statement, but they'll let me do that locally. They are sending someone here to talk to me and they will want to talk to Dante and the Dragons. My father's worried this might cause another problem for us," Bowie said. Mr. Wolfe was a smart man and he was right, Stinger's body showing up at Bowie's might cause more trouble for their new little family.

"I think it might be best if I'm the one who tells Dante about his guy. I'll send word that I want a meeting with him," Savage said.

"No fucking way you're going in there alone," Bowie growled. It was nice the way he seemed to worry about Savage, but honestly, he wanted to tell his guy that he was capable of taking care of himself in most situations.

"I've got this, Babe," Savage said. "But, if it makes you feel any better, I'll take Ryder along with me, just in case things go south." Bowie scowled at Savage and he knew that he was going to give him an argument.

"I can go with you," he insisted. There was no fucking way Savage wanted to drag Bowie into his world. Sure, having him around his club was one thing. His guys had come to accept Savage being with both Bowie and Dallas. But, introducing him to their rival gang didn't seem like his best idea.

"I need you to keep Dallas and the girls safe," Savage said. "I thought we covered this already. I need to know that if anything happens to me, you'll take care of them, Bowie. That's what family does."

"I don't need for you to lecture me about what a family is or does, Savage," Bowie grumbled. "Family also has each other's backs and you're not letting me tag along because you're worried I won't be able to handle myself," Bowie accused.

"Can you blame me? I love you, Bowie and I'd die if anything happened to you. Please, just do this for me," Savage begged.

"Fine," Bowie agreed. "You go have your meeting with Dante, but take back-up and be careful," he ordered. Savage gave him a mock salute and pulled him in for a quick kiss. He needed to get the meeting scheduled and round up a few guys to head over to Dragon's territory before his guy changed his mind.

SAVAGE KNEW that giving into Bowie and agreeing to take Ryder and Repo with him would be a mistake, so he didn't. He set up his meeting with Dante and when it came time to meet the guys at his bar, he lied and told them both that the meeting time had changed and Dante moved it to the next day. A little white lie, sure. But now, Savage worried it might cost him his life. Either way, it was time to get to the bottom of what the hell was going on. Not going into that bar to face Dante and the other Dragons he knew would be waiting for him, wasn't an option.

He parked his bike in the back of the lot and looked around, trying to decide if just walking in the front door was such a brilliant plan. Maybe the element of surprise might have been a better one, but it was too late for that now. Especially since the two big goons who were charged with watching the door, were walking straight for him. Yeah, his time for surprise was over and he had no choice but to face Dante full on.

"Guys," Savage nodded and tried to push past them on his way into Dante's bar, but they seemed to have other plans for him. The big guy to his right put his hand on Savage's bicep and he looked down at it as if it offended him and back up at the guy.

"I'll give you five seconds to take your fucking hand off me," Savage growled. Dante's enforcer ignored him as if Savage wasn't even a blip on his radar.

"Dante said to bring you in through the back of the bar," the other guy said. Savage looked over at him and smiled.

"What?" he questioned, "I'm not good enough to come through the front door anymore. I thought I was an invited guest of Dante's?" Savage said. Honestly, he was trying to buy some time. Taking on the two enforcers might not play in his favor. He was big but they were bigger and there were two of them. He knew that most of the bikers in Dante's club were one-percenters and taking him out might not be a problem for either of his escorts. The guy to his right, still holding his arm, flexed his giant fingers into Savage's flesh and that just pissed him off. Before he could think through his next move, he grabbed the guy's hand and pinned it behind his massive body, causing the asshole to shout out in pain.

"I told you to keep your fucking hands off me," Savage growled. The other man wrapped his big arm around Savage's neck, putting him in a chokehold and before he had the chance to tap out, he was being pinned against the guy's body. He knew what was coming next. The other guy's fist met his jaw, blood spurting everywhere. Savage spit out a mouthful of blood and smiled, knowing how mean he looked.

"So, this is how it's going to go then?" he asked. Neither guy made a move to answer him. They seemed to be waiting him out to see if he was going to give them any more fight. "Well let's get this over with," he barked. "Take me to Dante."

They practically dragged him into the back of the bar, even though Savage didn't put up much resistance. He just wanted to get this shit show over with. They led him through the kitchen and into the back of the bar, pushing him down into a hard wooden chair.

"Tie him up," Dante ordered. He stepped from the back corner of the bar and smiled at Savage. "How's it going, man?" he taunted.

"Oh, you know," Savage drawled. "Same old shit, different day." Dante's watchdogs tied him to the chair, punching him in the face for good measure, for his smart-ass answer. Savage chuckled and spat out more blood onto the bar's floor.

"I think you might want to look up the word 'truce,' Dante," Savage taunted. "You might have the meaning incorrect."

"Yeah, well," Dante laughed. "You really didn't buy my whole, 'let's be friends,' speech anyway, did you? We both know you're smarter than that, Savage. After all, you are literally a rocket scientist, right?" Dante pulled a chair across the floor, letting it make an obnoxious scraping noise. "Let's talk," Dante ordered.

"Well, looks like I'm sticking around," Savage said tugging against his restraints. "So, why not? Shoot," Savage ordered.

Dante chuckled and shook his head. He nodded to the big guy standing to Savage's right and he punched him in the damn face again. "Fuck," Savage swore.

"I have all night," Dante said. "How much we mess up that handsome face of yours is up to you," he said. "I just need some answers."

"Answers to what?" Savage growled.

"Answers about what the hell happened in Texas," Dante said. "My guy is dead and from what I've been hearing down the chains, you're the one who did it."

"I didn't kill Stinger," Savage shouted.

"Ah—but you know he's dead?" Dante questioned. Savage not only knew Stinger was dead, but he also had a pretty good idea who did it.

"Yeah," he admitted. "You know he had the word 'Traitor' carved into his chest?" He couldn't get a read on whether or not Dante knew that little bit of information.

"Well, shit," Dante said.

"Yeah, now you're getting the picture," Savage said. "One of Joker's guys found out and offed him. So, if we're done here—" Savage looked down to the ropes that bound him to the chair and Dante nodded at the big guy who stood to his left. He landed a deafening blow to the side of Savage's head, making his ears ring. It was all he could do to stay conscious.

"I don't know how you got your intel," Dante said, standing to pace in front of him. "But, you really went and fucked things up for me. Meet me outside," he said to the two guys who flanked Savage. "I'll be out in just a minute." They both left through the front door and Savage eyed Dante. "I can't have them around for this next part," Dante said.

"You don't have to do this," Savage said. "No one even knows about our meeting. I can just pretend none of this ever happened," he lied.

Dante laughed, "I'm not going to do anything, Savage. I have guys that do it all for me. For example," he paused, looking to his right and Savage noticed shadows moving in the dark crevices of the room that he hadn't noticed before. Joker and some of the supposedly 'rogue' Dragons stepped from the darkness and Savage squinted, trying to see them better.

"Hey, Savage," Joker taunted. "Long time, no see."

"What the fuck?" Savage growled. "They never went rogue, did they?" he accused.

"Naw," Dante admitted. "I had to make something up. I mean, not everyone in our club was happy about the decision to come after Savage Hell. They thought that years of our rival had been enough. I needed a distraction—you know some story to keep them in line. Joker here came up with the idea," Dante admitted.

"Thanks for the good word, man," Joker said. It was like they were at an office awards banquet, the way the two were giving each other props and Savage was just trying to wrap his head around the fact that it had all been a set- up.

"No problem, man. So, we came up with the whole rogue storyline to throw off the guys who were tired of our old feud. We got what we wanted without having to tear apart our club. Now, we'll pin Stinger's murder on you and these guys will be welcomed back into our gang with open arms. Hell, after we explain how you hunted and killed poor Sting, and then Joker here did the same thing to you—to exact revenge for the Dragons—he'll be labeled a fucking hero," Dante said.

Joker flexed his fingers and Savage knew what he had planned. They were going to kill him to make an example out of him, as a warning to his club. The problem was, he was a damn fool for going in alone. Bowie was right to insist that he take back-up, but he was a stubborn ass and he didn't listen.

"So, that's the plan? You're going to let Joker kill me and then tell everyone I killed Stinger? My guys won't believe that shit," he spat. Savage's ears were still ringing from the last blow landed to his head. He wasn't sure how much longer he'd be able to hold on. He could hear his own words slurring and it was getting harder to keep his damn eyes open.

"Yeah and from the looks of you, man, it won't take Joker here too long to finish the job. We don't give a fuck if your guys don't buy our story, man. All that matters here is that my guys believe it and want to continue our feud. I won't rest until every fucking member in Savage Hell is either a Dragon or completely fucking destroyed. Oh, and I've promised Joker here that he can keep your woman as his prize." Dante turned and nodded to Joker. He stood in front of Savage, his mean smile and bloodthirsty eyes told him all he needed to know. Joker was going to make him suffer and then finish the job Dante's enforcers started.

"The best part in all this is that I'll finally have your sweet little Dallas," Joker taunted. "I wasn't kidding when I said I wanted her back. I'll get rid of your brats and then I'll make Dallas mine." Savage bucked against his restraints, but it did him no good. He was too weak and no amount of resistance was going to free him from his bindings. "You'll have to find her first," Savage hoarsely whispered. "That will never happen."

Joker laughed, throwing the first punch that had Savage just about seeing stars. "I don't know," he said. I can be very persuasive when it comes to getting information," Joker taunted.

Savage saw Dallas' beautiful face flash through his mind, followed by Bowie's and his sweet girls' faces. Was this the way it was all going to end? They had just barely begun and now he was going to lose them. His only solace was knowing that Bowie would take care of Dallas and his girls. They were a family now and even if he was out of the equation, they'd find a way forward, together. Bowie would protect Dallas and the girls with his life and that was enough for Savage. He closed his eyes and let the darkness take him as Dante landed another blow to his battered jaw.

BOWIE

Bowie stood back in the shadows of the bar. He wasn't sure if Savage knew he was there or not, but he wouldn't take any chances by trying to get his attention. Joker stood in front of where Savage was tied to the chair, his knuckles red from Savage's blood. Bowie wanted to rush in there before the asshole got the chance to land another blow, but that would mean going in without back-up and he had a feeling that would end badly for both him and Savage. He just hoped like hell his guy could hold on for a few more minutes until Ryder and the other guys got there.

Bowie checked his watch and sent up a silent prayer that Dallas was able to reach Ryder and give him their location. He was pretty sure they were at the Dragon's clubhouse, but he couldn't be certain. Hell, he was just hoping their woman got the text he sent with all the details and Bowie realized that the calvary might not actually be showing up like he needed. There were a lot of unknown factors involved and he couldn't just stand by and let Savage get the shit beat out of him much longer. His guy looked pretty bad and Bowie wasn't sure just how much more he'd be able to take.

When he saw Savage sneak down to the bar after reading the girls their bedtime story, he knew his guy was up to no good. Savage usually came straight to bed after tucking the girls in for the night, so that the three of them could have their time together. Tonight, he had made some excuse about having to finish up an order for the bar and Bowie and Dallas knew better than to believe him. Savage had been acting squirrelly since Stinger's body showed up at Bowie's house in Texas. He couldn't shake the thought that Savage was going to go off and do something that might get him killed. Bowie hated that he was right, but none of that mattered right now. Savage was in bad shape and if he didn't figure something out fast, his guy wasn't going to make it.

Bowie followed Savage and when the two assholes dragged him in through the back door of the building, Bowie snuck in through a side door, hoping to escape any unwanted attention. The last thing either of them needed was for him to get caught trying to mount a one-man rescue attempt. He hadn't thought things through very well and now, all he could do was watch and wait—praying that Dallas got his text and was able to reach Ryder and Repo. They'd know what to do, even if he had no clue.

Bowie watched as Joker landed one punishing blow after another. Savage wavered in and out of consciousness and just when he thought his guy wouldn't be able to stand another hit, he'd wake up and mumble another slight that had Joker pissed and punching the shit out of Savage. Bowie wanted to tell him to shut the fuck up and stay down; hoping that would end his torment. Dante whispered something to Joker and left the bar. All but two guys and Joker left with him. Bowie liked the odds a little better now, but he couldn't be sure that there weren't more guys outside the bar.

"This can all end here and now," Joker growled. "Just tell us where to find my girl and we'll let you go."

Savage's smile was mean. "Go fuck yourself," he offered. Bowie braced himself, knowing that Savage's defiance was going to earn him more of a beating.

"Shit," Bowie said under his breath. Joker pulled his arm back and threw another punch, landing it square on Savage's already bloody jaw.

"That all you got?" Savage taunted. Bowie wanted to tell him to shut the fuck up, but that wasn't who Savage was. He was going to give the big goon as much shit as possible.

"I just want my girl back, asshole. You can't just decide to be a part of her life again and take her back." Joker grumbled.

"I can and I did. She was never yours, Joker," Savage slurred. "She's always been mine. You two went on what, one date?" he taunted.

"We had a connection," Joker screamed. This lunatic believed that Dallas wanted to be with him and that Savage was standing in his way. Joker was unstable and Bowie worried Savage's taunts weren't helping matters.

The two guys who had helped Savage into the bar appeared from the back room. Bowie assumed there was a kitchen back there, but he couldn't see past the back wall of the bar. The smaller of the two guys walked up to Joker and handed him a set of keys. "We found these on his bike. They might be keys to his house and we're betting she's staying with him," he said, handing them to Joker. Bowie knew the keys would get Joker and his guys into their house. He just prayed that Dallas had gotten his message and they wouldn't find her there.

"You stay the fuck away from her," Savage spat. Joker smiled back at the two other guys.

"I think we just got our answer," he said. "Round up the guys and tell them we ride in ten minutes. The sooner we get there, the sooner I can claim my sweet Dallas." He looked back down at Savage and laughed. "How does it feel, knowing that I'm going to take my woman back from you and make her mine? This time, I won't let her tell me no." The thought of that asshole laying one finger on Dallas made Bowie sick. Judging by the angry scowl on Savage's face, he felt the exact same way.

"You touch Dallas and I'll tear you apart," Savage warned. The three guys laughed at him and turned to go back into the room behind the bar. "Come back here," Savage yelled. "Don't you fucking touch her." The back door slammed and Bowie didn't make a move towards where Savage sat bound to a chair. He worried that it was a trap and that one of the guys would be back in. Would they really just leave Savage tied to a chair while they went to find Dallas?

"Fuck," Savage swore.

Bowie heard the sound of engines revving in the parking lot, just outside, and he held his breath hoping that they had just gotten lucky. He waited, listening for the sound of motorcycles roaring down the street to fade into complete silence.

"Savage," Bowie whispered. Savage's head dipped as if he had nodded off. He was pretty beat up and seemed to be having trouble staying awake. "Savage," he said again.

"Bowie?" Savage questioned. "Are you really here?"

"Yeah, man," Bowie said. "I had to be sure they're gone. I think we're in the clear."

"Untie me," Savage demanded. "We have to get to Dallas before they do."

"We need to call the cops," Bowie said. "I know you said you don't want the cops involved in this mess, but we have no choice now." He worked Savage's hands loose from their bindings and Savage pulled them free, rubbing the feeling back into them.

"Thanks, man," he said. "I did say that, but we have no choice. We can't let them get to Dallas and the girls. They already killed one of their own guys, I won't let them hurt anyone else. I won't take that risk. We have enough evidence to put most of them away. Make the call." Bowie nodded and pulled out his cell. He called 911 and told them where they'd be able to find the Dragons. He hated that this shit storm was going to go down at their home, but he really had no other choice. When he ended the call, he found Savage slumped against the wall. "I think I have a concussion, man," he slurred. "Call Ryder and give him a heads-up about what's about to go down. I want as many of our guys out at the house protecting Dallas and the girls as possible." Bowie smiled. His guy was bossy even with being beaten within an inch of his life. He wrapped an arm around Savage's waist and helped him back to the chair.

"Sit," he ordered. "I'll call Ryder and make sure our girls are safe." He took Savage's phone and found Ryder's contact information, calling his cell. Bowie quickly told Ryder what was going on watching as Savage nodded in and out of consciousness. Bowie needed to get him to the hospital and have him checked out.

"We don't have many guys still here at Savage Hell," Ryder said. "By the time I call everyone back, the Dragons will be here."

"Shit," Bowie cursed. He had to think fast otherwise Dallas and the girls were going to be right in the middle of a shit storm. He couldn't let that happen. "Get them out of there. I don't want them tied to the Dragons and the last thing we need is a showdown at Savage Hell. Move everyone over to Repo's house, including Dallas and the girls. Don't let them out of your sight until I get there," Bowie ordered and ended his call.

"We have to get you to a hospital," Bowie said. Savage tried to protest, but Bowie wasn't having it. He helped Savage up from his chair and they had almost found their way out the back of the bar when the front door flew open. Bowie turned in time to find one of the little guys who he believed to be Joker's right-hand man, walking in as if he was on a mission. The poor guy looked a little confused, not finding Savage just where Joker had left him, tied to the chair.

"What the fuck," he barked. Bowie pulled his gun from his shoulder holster, pointing it at the guy. He reached for his piece, and Bowie shouted at him to stop.

"Don't even think about it, fucker." The guy looked as if he was weighing his options and Bowie chuckled. "Seriously, I can tell you're thinking about it. Doesn't he look like he's thinking about reaching for his gun, Savage?" Savage weakly nodded and made a humming noise.

"He does," Savage agreed. "He's a dumb fucker, though. He probably isn't smart enough to know that you are military trained and can blow his fucking head off before he even gets his gun out of his waistband." Bowie tightened his arm around Savage's waist. He wasn't sure if he'd be able to keep a hold on his guy and take down this asshole at the same time, but he was going to give it one hell of a try.

"He's right," Bowie agreed. "How about you try to use some of those brain cells and make the right decision here, dude. I'd hate to have to waste a bullet on you." The asshole stuck his hands in the air as if he was going to surrender, but

Bowie could see it in his eyes—he had no plans on doing any such thing.

"Shit," Bowie growled. The guy reached behind him, pulling the gun from his waistband and Bowie pulled the trigger, putting a bullet between his eyes.

"Bullseye," Savage whispered. "Just like I said. You good, man?" he questioned. Bowie leaned Savage against the wall and crossed the bar to make sure the guy was dead, kicking his weapon away from his hand, just in case.

"I had no choice," he defended.

"No," Savage agreed. "You didn't." Bowie shoved his gun back into its holster and pulled out his cell.

"What are you doing?" Savage asked.

"I'm calling this in," he said. Savage stood a little straighter and Bowie could tell he was going to give him a fight.

"No," Savage said. "You aren't here. No one will ever know that you were here. I'll tell them that I was the one who shot him. I took your gun from home and when he came into the bar to kill me, I got loose from my bindings and shot him." Savage weakly crossed the bar and took the gun from Bowie. "One in the chest," he said, firing the gun at the dead guy's chest and once in the head." Savage put the gun in his own waistband.

"No," Bowie protested.

"It's the only way. They beat the shit out of me and wanted me dead. It was self-defense. This asshole came in to kill me in cold blood and I just beat him to the punch," Savage smiled and winced at the pain it must have caused. "The cops won't dig too deep on this one, Babe. It'll be considered a turf war and I'll be fine. Give me my cell so I can call this in. You get back to our woman and keep our family safe. The cops should be headed to our house already from your earlier call. Go be with Dallas and help her through all this. I'll be fine," Savage lied.

Bowie nodded, not quite sure he believed a word Savage was saying. It felt like they were in the center of a shitstorm and he worried they wouldn't be able to find their way clear. Especially not now with a dead Dragon on their hands.

BOWIE COULDN'T DRIVE his damn pick-up truck fast enough back to their house. He called Dallas as soon as he left Savage, to tell her what was going on. Hearing the panic and fear in her voice nearly did him in. He couldn't get home to her fast enough. She said that the cops had shown up at the same time as the Dragons. Dallas stayed on the phone with him while they waited to see if Joker and his guys were going to stand down. Bowie felt as though he was holding his fucking breath, waiting for Dallas to tell him that she was safe.

"They gave up," Dallas' voice broke and Ryder must have taken the phone from her.

"Hey, man," he said." Joker surrendered and the cops are cuffing him and his crew now. You and Savage good?" Ryder asked. That was the million-dollar question. Bowie wasn't sure they were and it took all his willpower not to break down on the phone with Ryder.

"I don't know, man," Bowie said. "Savage is waiting for the cops to show up at Dante's. A guy's dead and I just left him."

"I know," Ryder said," Savage called me and gave me the details. He's going to be taken in and checked over. They seem to have bought the whole self-defense story."

"I need to be with him," Bowie said.

"No," Ryder insisted. "You need to do what Savage

ordered you to do and get your ass back here. Dallas and the girls are shook up and you need to take care of your woman." Bowie quietly nodded, knowing Ryder couldn't see him. He was right, it was what Savage had told him to do. His responsibility was to Dallas and the girls. He'd get them settled and then he'd make sure his guy was alright.

"I'll be back home in five minutes," Bowie agreed. "Just keep them safe until then," he ordered.

"Will do," Ryder agreed. "Be safe, man."

"Always," Bowie breathed.

It had been two weeks of Savage being called down to the local police station for questioning. Each time he left, Dallas ended up in Bowie's arms, sobbing uncontrollably with worry. He had to admit, he was beginning to worry that this whole mess would never end. Dante had disappeared, with most of his club in tow. Savage had heard a rumor that they had crossed the border into Mexico, but he had a hard time believing that they would just leave all their interest unprotected and disappear. Dante was a major player in most of the town's seedier businesses. There were rumors he had a decent sized human trafficking ring going and it was a well-known fact that he ran drugs and prostitutes through Huntsville on a regular basis. He had a lucrative business and Savage said there would be no way he'd walk away from it to hide down in Mexico. Bowie trusted Savage's gut, but a part of him hoped his guy was wrong about all of it.

Savage walked into the kitchen and threw his keys down on the table. "I'm done," he almost whispered.

"Come again," Bowie asked.

"I'm done," he repeated. "They are finished questioning

me and I'm free and clear." Dallas crossed the kitchen and threw her arms around Savage's neck.

"Really?" she questioned. "We are free?"

"Yep," he said, flexing his big hands into her curvy ass. "We're free." Bowie smiled and framed Dallas' back, wrapping his arms around the both of them. He felt a little less relieved than the other two seemed to feel about the whole situation. He wasn't sure they would ever be free, as long as Dante and his club were still out there. He had heard Dante tell Savage that night at his bar, that he wouldn't rest until every last member of Savage Hell was either a Dragon or dead. Now, that would include him and Bowie knew that sooner or later he'd have to tell Dallas and Savage his news.

"You don't seem as happy about all this, Babe," Savage chided.

"Well, I've been waiting to tell you guys my news and I'm not sure how you will both take it," Bowie said, changing the subject.

"What news?" Dallas questioned.

"Shit," Savage growled. "Tell me the murmurs I've heard around my club aren't fucking true, Bowie," Savage ordered. Bowie knew that news of him prospecting for Savage Hell would eventually get back to Savage. He was the club's president and nothing got past him. Ryder had agreed to let Bowie be the one to break the news to him, even though that went against club rules. The sponsor was the one who usually introduced the prospect to the club's president, but in this case, Savage and Bowie knew each other quite well.

"Yeah," Bowie said. "I'm prospecting and Ryder is my sponsor."

"Fuck," Savage barked. "Why am I not hearing this from Ryder?" he questioned.

SAVAGE HEAT

"Ryder agreed to let me be the one to tell you," Bowie said.

"That's not how this is done, Babe," Savage countered.

"Well, I'm sure it's not, but I'm also pretty sure that the president isn't usually fucking his club's prospect either," Bowie countered.

"Shit," Savage grumbled.

"I know that this is fucked up, man, but I want to do this. You and Dallas are my lives now and I want to be a part of them in every way. I love your club, Savage and I want to be a part of that family. They've accepted the three of us together and I don't know, it just feels like the next logical step." Savage seemed to be thinking it all over and Dallas turned to face him.

"Well, I for one, think it's a great idea," she said. "I'm not sure what to say here—congratulations? Go get 'em?" Dallas giggled and Bowie kissed her.

"Thanks, Baby," he said. "How about it, man? Do I get to prospect?" Bowie knew that as club president, Savage would have the final say. He just hoped like hell he'd give him a chance because Bowie wanted nothing more than to be a part of the Savage Hell family.

Savage sighed, "Yeah," he grumbled.

"Thanks, Savage," Bowie said. He kissed him, squeezing Dallas between the two of them and Bowie wasn't sure how he'd gotten so lucky. Just months earlier, he was following the sexy, brooding Savage around base, trying to figure out a way to get the guy to notice him. Now, he was in love with not one, but two people he was sure he'd never find.

"Don't thank me yet, Bowie," Savage insisted. "As a prospect of Savage Hell, I'll own your ass." Dallas broke out into fits of giggles between the two of them.

"What's so funny, Baby?" Bowie asked.

"Um, I think he already owns your ass, Bowie," Dallas teased. Bowie looked at Savage who was trying and failing to hide his smile.

"Well, she's not wrong," Savage growled.

"No, she's not," Bowie said. Yeah, he was one lucky son-of-a-bitch.

DALLAS

T hree Months Later

DALLAS SAT in Savage's office, waiting for the guys to get home. They were driving back from their quick trip to Texas to help Bowie's parents move into their new condo. He had spent the last few months convincing his mom to give up her beloved home and his dad was relieved that they were finally going to be able to slow down.

She was supposed to go with them, but when she woke up sick again the day before, she backed out of their trip. Dallas had been battling the stomach virus for a couple of weeks now and her biggest fear was Greer or Chloe catching it from her. The guys had picked up the slack around the house, giving her extra time to rest and recuperate, but she was starting to think that she wasn't contagious. If her hunch was correct, she had something else to worry about and telling the guys might be the worst of it. Dallas had been sick like this one other time in her life when she was pregnant with Greer. She worried that telling the guys that she was pregnant again might be harder than losing her breakfast every morning.

Savage had called to check in on her about an hour ago and told her that they'd be home soon. Dallas called the girls' sitter and had her come out to the house and ran down to the bar. She texted them both to meet her there and told Whisky to send them back to the office once they got in. She liked the new guy and was hoping he'd stick around. She saw something in him that reminded her a lot of herself. Dallas was hoping that sooner or later he'd open up and let one of them in, but so far that hadn't happened. He kept to himself and held onto his privacy like it was all he had left.

Savage peeked into his office and she swiveled around in his big chair. "Hey," Dallas whispered. She cleared her throat and stood, stretching from sitting in one position for so long. Savage let his eyes roam her body and she giggled.

"Well, that was a nice welcome," Savage teased. Bowie walked into the small office, crowding into the room next to Savage.

"Hey Baby, what did I miss?" he asked. Savage dropped his duffel bag and pulled Dallas against his body.

"Dallas was just reminding me how much I missed her." Savage kissed her and Dallas didn't hesitate to wrap her arms around his neck, to pull him down for more. She could feel the heat coming from Bowie's body as he crowded up behind her.

"My turn, Honey," he demanded. Savage turned her in his arms, pressing her back to his front, letting her feel his erection against her ass.

"Kiss our guy, Baby," Savage ordered. "Show him how

much you missed him." Dallas loved the way Savage seemed to need to take charge of them both. She knew he was bossy, but the three of them together seemed to ramp up his need for control. Bowie kissed and licked his way into her mouth, doing exactly as Savage ordered.

"She tastes so fucking good," Bowie growled.

Savage hummed his approval, "It's so hot watching the two of you together," he said.

"I like watching you both, too," Dallas admitted. It never got old seeing Bowie and Savage kissing. When Savage pushed her and Bowie together, she wasn't sure how the three of them would work. Dallas worried that she would be jealous of seeing Savage with anyone else—man or woman. But, she never felt that way. She had fallen in love with them both and now, she couldn't imagine her life any differently. Telling the guys that they were going to be daddies again shouldn't worry her. She knew she was being silly especially with the way they seemed to divvy up being fathers to the girls.

Dallas was in awe of just how accepting Chloe had been of Bowie. She had even started calling him "Daddy" and Dallas could tell that every time Bowie heard her say his name, he melted just a little more. That little girl had them both wrapped around her finger and Dallas couldn't fault the guys. She was a special little girl and Dallas hoped that someday Chloe would even consider her to be a mother figure for her. She had slipped up a couple of times and called her "Mommy" but then she'd quickly corrected herself. Dallas hoped that one day Chloe would let her be that for her, but she'd be patient and let that happen on Chloe's terms.

"So," Savage said, interrupting her thoughts, "why did you want to meet us here?" he questioned.

"Um, I wanted to talk to you both and I didn't want to do it back at the house. Little ears and all," she teased.

"Yeah, our girls do make it hard to have an adult conversation," Bowie agreed. "Is that what we're having here, Honey?" Bowie kissed his way down her neck and she could feel her heart racing, sure he'd be able to feel her pulse in her neck.

"Well, it is an adult conversation," she stuttered, trying to keep up with both her guys, but when they were touching and kissing her like this it was always a challenge.

"Thank fuck," Savage growled against her skin. "How about we get to the part where we do adult things to you too, Baby?"

Dallas pushed at their big bodies as if that would do her any good. "Guys," she chided. "I can't think straight when you do this to me."

"Okay, how about you let us do all the thinking," Bowie teased.

"This is important," she reprimanded.

"I like it when you get all testy, Honey," Savage said. "It makes me hot when you reprimand us."

"Savage," she squeaked when he reached around her body to grab a handful of her ass. "I'm pregnant," she shouted. Both guys immediately stopped pawing and kissing her and the look on both of their faces was almost comical.

"What?" Bowie asked. "Pregnant?"

"Um, yeah," Dallas said. "As in, I'm going to have a baby."

"Our baby?" Savage asked, pointing between both him and Bowie.

"Well, I'm not sure who else you think I've been sleeping with, Savage," she teased. "Please believe I didn't plan this. Hell, I don't seem to be very good with the whole planned pregnancy thing. I think a surprise baby is more my thing."

Dallas knew she was rambling, but that's what she did when she was nervous and for some crazy reason, she was nervous about telling the guys she was going to have a baby.

"Are you sure?" Savage asked. "I mean, did you take a test?" She was going to wait for them to get home, but Dallas gave up the fight and about thirty minutes ago, she took a pregnancy test. She was just too much of a chicken to go back into the bathroom to look at the results.

"Yes," she said. "It's in your bathroom." She pointed to the door behind her. "I didn't have the guts to check the results for myself. But, I'm having all the same symptoms that I had with Greer. I ignored them for as long as humanly possible, but it's time to face facts—I think I'm pregnant again."

"Okay," Bowie soothed. "How about we go in and check the test out together. Let's not get ahead of ourselves here."

"I, for one, am happy you're pregnant," Savage said. "Are you happy about the baby, Honey?" Dallas wasn't sure how she felt about a new baby. She was just starting to adjust to it being the five of them. Sure, she'd love the new baby, but was she happy about him or her?

"Yes," she whispered. "I think that I am happy about this baby. I love Greer and Chloe so much. I know we're all so new to each other still, but this just feels like the next step."

"I agree," Bowie said. "If that test is positive, I'll be thrilled and if it's not, I say we start trying to make one anyway." Dallas smiled and nodded.

"So, we're doing this then? Having a baby?" Savage asked.

She nodded, "One way or another," Dallas agreed.

"Wait here," Bowie ordered and disappeared into Savage's private bathroom. He returned seconds later holding up the pregnancy test, wearing a triumphant grin.

"Well, it looks like we're having a baby," he said. Dallas covered her mouth, trying to hide the sob that escaped.

"Hey," Savage soothed. "This is a good thing, remember?"

"It is," she agreed. Dallas wiped at her hot tears that spilled down her face. "These are happy tears." She wasn't sure how she had gotten so lucky with her guys, but she knew not to question fate. Somehow, someway, the universe had thrown the three of them together and Dallas wasn't sure how she had ever coped without her guys. They were her Royal Bastards and she was their queen—now and forever.

EPILOGUE

SAVAGE

S avage sat in the holding cell, waiting for the officers to bring Cillian in to see him. He knew his old friend would call him for help sooner or later. Cillian James was the one he failed and Savage lived with that disappointment in himself every damn day. Savage was good friends with Cillian's dad and had been since they arrived from Ireland, when Cillian was just a kid. He promised to keep an eye on him after his parents went back to Ireland and Cillian stayed in the U.S., but somewhere along the line, Savage failed him.

When Cillian tried to join Savage's MC, he refused him. Patching in the kid would have been the wrong call. He didn't belong in that group of military misfits and one-percenters who made up his motley crew. To Savage, they were family but to Cillian, they would mean the end of what he wanted—a chance at a normal life. So, he told the kid that he didn't want him and even made up some excuse about

181

him being too hot-tempered for their club, just to throw him off the scent. It had the opposite effect though and Cillian became even more determined to find his way in. Even if that meant joining Savage Hell's rival club—the Dragons. They were bad news and before Savage could step in and save Cillian, he had stolen a car to try to prove his worth to the Dragons. The problem was—they didn't really want Cillian and when it came down to it, they let him rot in prison over a gang prank that went wrong.

Their leader thought it would be funny to set Cillian up to take the fall for grand theft auto and he took the bait and was now serving his time for the crime he committed. It pissed Savage off knowing that he could have prevented all of Cillian's problems if he had just let him into Savage Hell. But, it was too late to go back and change all of that. All Savage could do now was help his friend and he was hoping that was why he was summoned to the prison so early on a Monday morning.

The steel door creaked open and Cillian walked in wearing handcuffs and a smile. The officer instructed them that they were not allowed any physical contact, they only had ten minutes for their visit, and asked Savage if he wanted Cillian's cuffs on or off.

"Off," Savage growled. As soon as the handcuffs were off, Cillian sat down on the other side of the table from Savage and nodded.

"Thanks for coming, man," Cillian said.

"No problem, Cillian. It's been a damn long time," Savage said. "I've been here a few times, but you refused to see me— what was up with that, man?"

Cillian chuckled and Savage sat back to cross his arms over his chest, finding the whole thing less funny than his friend.

"You haven't changed a bit," Cillian said and Savage just shrugged. "It's been a long time since I heard anyone call me by my real name. I was starting to forget who I was in here."

"Yeah, I heard about all of that," Savage said. "You got into some trouble. I heard you killed a man." Cillian eyed the guard who stood in the corner of the room, watching and listening to every word they were saying.

"Nope," he said. "But, I got the credit in the yard for it and that's how I got my nickname—Kill." Cillian flashed Savage a grin and he shook his head.

"It doesn't suit you," Savage growled. "I think I'll stick with your real name, Cillian." His friend didn't seem at all put off by him refusing to use his new nickname, even shrugging it off.

"Suit yourself," he said, his Irish accent sounded in full. Savage didn't realize just how much he had missed his friend until just now.

"It's good to see you," Savage whispered. "So much has happened since you've been in here."

"Yeah well, ten years is a damn long time. And, I'm sorry about turning you away when you came to visit but I just couldn't see you. Knowing you were here for me was enough but seeing you would have pained me. I would have longed for a life that I could never have." Cillian's expression was bitter and Savage realized that the boy he used to know wasn't sitting across the table from him. Cillian had become the man that prison had made him. He truly was 'Kill' now but Savage refused to believe he couldn't have the life he wanted, once he got out of that awful place.

"Why am I here now?" Savage asked, cutting straight to the chase. The guard was watching the clock and he knew that their ten minutes were just about up. It was time to find out why Cillian wanted to see him now after so much time had passed.

"I'm getting out," Cillian breathed.

"That's great, man," Savage said. "When?"

"Probably sometime next week. The date hasn't been set yet but my lawyer said it's a done deal. I need an advocate on the outside," Cillian all but whispered. "I was hoping it would be you."

"Of course, anything you need, man," Savage offered and he meant it too.

"I can't be around any felons, as part of my parole conditions," Cillian said. Savage nodded his understanding.

"So, no Savage Hell party at the clubhouse to welcome you home then?" Cillian smiled.

"No," he agreed. "I really appreciate the club taking me under its wing after I did what I did with the Dragons. Savage Hell and you have had my back through all of this, but I can't be around most of the guys while I'm on parole."

Savage laughed, "Yeah, they aren't really the upstanding citizens your parole officer will want you hanging around with, I'm afraid," he said. "But, you have my help—whatever you need."

"Can you pick me up and help me find a place to live and maybe a job, once I get sprung?" Cillian asked. He fidgeted with his own hands on the metal desk and for just a minute, Savage caught a glimpse of the shy boy who came from Ireland and didn't quite fit in anywhere.

"Of course," Savage said. "Consider it done."

"How's the family? I got your letters about Bowie and Dallas—I'm so happy for you, man," Cillian said. Savage wasn't sure if he believed him or not. He could hear the undertones of sadness in Cillian's voice.

"You'll get there too, Cillian. Someday—"

"Don't," Cillian barked. "Don't give me hope for someday, Savage. It hurts too much to think about not having that happiness in my life—a wife, kids—a family. It's not for me now so don't feed me some bullshit about someday," he growled. Savage nodded, knowing that now wasn't the time to argue with his friend. Not when their precious time was ticking down to mere seconds.

"That's time," the guard called. "Let's go, Kill." Cillian stood as ordered and nodded to Savage.

"I'll be here when you get out, Cillian," Savage promised.

"Thanks, man," Cillian said. The guard put the cuffs back on him and he turned to leave the room. "I knew I could count on you, Savage."

CILLIAN

Kill had been counting down the days to his release and what was promised to be only one week away, ended up being two. When the day finally arrived for him to be released, Savage was waiting for him just outside the prison gates as promised. He was the one guy Kill could count on and he had to admit that it felt damn good to have someone on his side for a change.

During his exit interview with his parole officer, he was quickly reminded about the fact that most inmates end up right back in prison after they were let out. Kill didn't want to believe he could so easily end up as a statistic, but it was his biggest fear.

"Hey, man," Savage said, pulling him in for a quick hug. "You look good."

"Yeah, thanks for sending in some clothes for me. The ones they had of mine, from ten years ago, weren't exactly going to fit." Savage looked him up and down as if sizing him up. He was just a kid when he went to prison for grand theft auto—just twenty-three. It seemed like a lifetime ago.

"No," Savage said. "I guess they wouldn't. You have filled out in the last ten years."

Kill laughed, "Yep. Not much else to do in prison besides lift and workout."

"Well, I have a few bags of clothes in the trunk. Nothing fancy, just some stuff the guys got together and my girl loves to shop. Dallas had a field day picking you up some clothes. She even guessed your size and got you a suit, you know—for job interviews and stuff."

"I appreciate it, Savage. I'll find a way to pay you back," Kill promised.

Savage pointed his finger at Kill. "No, you won't. We're family and family takes care of each other," he said. "Now, get in. We need to get this apartment hunting underway. Until we can find you something, you'll be staying with me and my family. I've already given your parole officer my address and cell number." Savage got into the cab of his black pick-up and Kill slid into the passenger seat. He handed Kill a cell phone and he turned it over in his hand. He had never really had his own cell phone and wasn't sure how to work the new ones. He only ever used the ones that flipped open but this one didn't have that feature.

"Push the side button and it turns on. It's charged and I've added you to my family plan," Savage said.

"This is too much, Savage," Kill whispered. It was too. He had forgotten what it meant to have family around and Savage treating him like a kid brother made him homesick for something that didn't exist anymore.

Kill's parents announced they were moving to the States when he was nineteen. They offered to bring him along but leaving Ireland felt like he was cutting off one of his own appendages. He reluctantly agreed to follow them across the pond but Ireland was a part of him and he still longed to go back. But now, he had nothing and no one to go back to. His parents returned home, to Ireland just after he turned twenty-one, and he foolishly decided to stay in America. He was trying to get into Savage's MC—Savage Hell and he thought he was too good to go back to his childhood roots. He told his father that he wanted to stay in America and make something of himself, even implying his dad couldn't hack it in the States. God, he was an asshole. His father convinced Savage to keep an eye on him and his parents headed back to Ireland.

About three months later, he got the call from his Mum that his father had died. He had a heart attack in his sleep and she found him dead the next morning. He didn't even go home for the funeral, even though his mother begged him to. Savage offered to lend him the money, but a mix of pride and being a stubborn ass took over and he refused. It was one of his major regrets and now that he was looking back, probably the one thing that shoved him down the wrong path. His life seemed to spiral out of control after his dad passed and one wrong decision led to the next and before he knew it, Kill was sitting behind the wheel of a stolen car, trying to prove he was worth something.

He begged Savage to let him into Savage Hell. Kill showed up to the bar that housed the club almost daily and each and every time Savage denied him; it drove him further over the line. When the Dragons showed interest in him, he jumped at the chance to be a part of a motorcycle club. He thought he'd show Savage just what he was made of by joining the Dragons and then he'd let him into Savage Hell. He was an idiot—he knew that now. But, at the time, it seemed like such a great plan. It wasn't and that point hit home when he realized his new club set him up. They knew he was mixed up with Savage and they used him to send Savage Hell a message. Dante was the president of the Dragons and he told Kill that if he wanted to be patched in, he needed to steal a car and bring it to the meeting. He wanted to be a part of something so badly he didn't think through the ramifications and getting caught seemed like a risk worth taking. He didn't even get a half a mile down the road with the car he stole before the cops pulled him over. During his hearing, it came out that he was set-up by the Dragons who were cooperating fully with the authorities. The judge decided to make an example out of him and gave Kill a twelve-year sentence, of which he served ten and with good behavior, got out.

About a year ago, he got a letter from his aunt in Ireland, telling him that his Mum had passed from cancer. He didn't even know she had the disease and it just about broke his heart that he didn't get to say goodbye to her. After his sentencing, she wrote him a letter, telling him that she would always love him, but that would be the last he'd ever hear from her and she was a woman who was true to her word.

"You good, Cillian?" Savage asked.

"Yeah," he lied. "Just thinking about everything. This is all a lot to take in," he admitted.

"Give it time, brother. You will have to do a lot of adjusting, but I believe in you, man. You need help, you use that to call me," Savage ordered, nodding to the cell phone Kill was clutching like it was his lifeline.

"Will do," Kill agreed. "And, thanks, Savage."

"Don't thank me yet, Cillian. You're bunking with the new baby and he'll keep you up all damn night long." Savage laughed.

"Remember, I've been in prison for the last ten years. Rooming with a newborn will be a piece of cake," Kill said.

"Yeah, we'll see if you're humming the same tune tomorrow morning when he wakes you up at four A.M.,

man," Savage said. "Welcome to the family, Cillian." Savage had no idea what those words meant to him and Cillian swallowed past the lump of emotion in his throat. It felt damn good to have a family again—now he just needed to find his place in the world—his home.

THE END

TO BE CONTINUED IN ROADKILL (SAVAGE HELL BOOK 1)
Coming May 2020!

ABOUT K.L. RAMSEY & BE KELLY

Romance Rebel fighting for
Happily Ever After!

K. L. Ramsey currently resides in West Virginia (Go Mountaineers!). In her spare time, she likes to read romance novels, go to WVU football games and attend book club (aka-drink wine) with girlfriends. K. L. enjoys writing Contemporary Romance, Erotic Romance, and Sexy Ménage! She loves to write strong, capable women and bossy, hot as hell alphas, who fall ass over tea kettle for them. And of course, her stories always have a happy ending. But wait—there's more!

Somewhere along the writing path, K.L. developed a love of ALL things paranormal (but has a special affinity for shifters <YUM!!>)!! She decided to take a chance and create another persona- BE Kelly- to bring you all of her yummy shifters, seers, and everything paranormal (plus a hefty dash of MC!).

K. L. RAMSEY'S SOCIAL MEDIA

Ramsey's Rebels - K.L. Ramsey's Readers Group
https://www.facebook.com/groups/ramseysrebels

KL Ramsey & BE Kelly's ARC Team
https://www.facebook.com/
groups/klramseyandbekellyarcteam

KL Ramsey and BE Kelly's Newsletter
https://mailchi.mp/4e73ed1b04b9/authorklramsey/

KL Ramsey and BE Kelly's Website
https://www.klramsey.com

facebook.com/kl.ramsey.58
instagram.com/itsprivate2
bookbub.com/profile/k-l-ramsey
twitter.com/KLRamsey5

BE KELLY'S SOCIAL MEDIA

BE Kelly's Reader's group
https://www.facebook.com/
groups/kellsangelsreadersgroup/

facebook.com/be.kelly.564

instagram.com/bekellyparanormalromanceauthor

twitter.com/BEKelly9

bookbub.com/profile/be-kelly

MORE WORKS BY K. L. RAMSEY

The Relinquished Series Boxed Set (Coming soon)

Love Times Infinity

Love's Patient Journey

Love's Design

Love's Promise

Harvest Ridge Series Box Set

Worth the Wait

The Christmas Wedding

Line of Fire

Torn Devotion

Fighting for Justice

Last First Kiss Series Box Set

Theirs to Keep

Theirs to Love

Theirs to Have

Theirs to Take

Second Chance Summer Series

True North

The Wrong Mister Right

Ties That Bind Series

Saving Valentine

Blurred Lines

Dirty Little Secrets

Taken Series

Double Bossed

Double Crossed

Owned

His Secret Submissive

His Reluctant Submissive

His Cougar Submissive

His Nerdy Submissive (Coming soon)

Alphas in Uniform

Hellfire

His Destiny (Coming soon)

Royal Bastards MC

Savage Heat

Whiskey Tango (Coming soon)

Savage Hell MC Series

Roadkill

REPOssession

Dirty Ryder (Coming soon)

Girl Power Romance Series/Scarlet Letter Series

Hard Limits (Coming soon)

No Limits (Coming soon)

Dirty Desire Series

Torrid (Coming soon)

Smokey Bandits MC Series

Aces Wild (Coming soon)

Mountain Men Mercenary Series (Coming soon)

WORKS BY BE KELLY (K.L.'S ALTER EGO...)

Reckoning MC Seer Series

Reaper

Tank

Raven

Perdition MC Shifter Series

Ringer

Rios

Trace

Wren's Pack (Coming soon)

Silver Wolf Shifter Series

Daddy Wolf's Little Seer (Coming soon)

Demonic Retribution Series

Sinner (Coming soon)

Graystone Academy Series (Coming soon)

Made in the USA
Middletown, DE
15 February 2022